SHE WAS AT HIS MERCY—

At the mercy of the cold night and her own inner longing.

"Get in," he said almost tonelessly. "But first take off your jeans. They'll be too uncomfortable to wear inside the sleeping bag."

Phoebe's fingers went reluctantly to the button on her jeans and she stepped out of them under the shelter of the blanket. For once in her life she felt absolutely helpless to resist the will of a man and it was both frightening and exhilarating. Harlan watched her, never taking his eyes from her face. A moment later she slid down beside him, reveling in the warmth and fearing the worst.

"This is much better than the floor, isn't it?" he asked.

"It's warmer," she agreed in a tiny voice as she lay curled into the heat of his body.

"And more comfortable?" he suggested coolly, daring her to disagree.

"Yes," she responded stiffly.

"You're wondering what happens next, aren't you?" he persisted wickedly.

"Yes." The words were barely a whisper.

"You," he informed her with a soft, mocking smile, "are just going to have to trust me!"

JAYNE ANN KRENTZ

**WRITING AS
JAYNE TAYLOR**

WHIRLWIND COURTSHIP

LEISURE BOOKS ∞ NEW YORK CITY

A LEISURE BOOK

Published by

Dorchester Publishing Co., Inc.
6 East 39th Street
New York, NY 10016

Printed in the United States of America

chapter one

It was six o'clock in the morning when Phoebe Hampton finally managed to stumble into a clearing in the Oregon woods and spotted the cabin. She had been picking her way steadily along the bank of the stream for two hours, growing hungrier with each step. The promising fragrance of a wood fire had been assailing her sensitive, if rather ordinary-looking nose for the past fifteen minutes. It had driven her to feats of somewhat reckless abandon such as sliding down an outcropping of boulders instead of going around them and nearly tromping through a patch of poison oak before spotting it. The last had made her wonder how much of the stuff she had plowed into in the first panicked flight during the night. Well, it couldn't be helped. She vowed to wash her hands before touching her face, however.

The face she was trying to protect from an unpleasant rash was a reasonable frame for the nose. Phoebe had always thought a little sadly that her face was rather ordinary and not at all the type which caused men to turn around for a second look. Still, Richard seemed contented with it. She had no notion of how a beautifully lashed set of blue-green eyes which regarded the world with a lively intelligence set off her features to the more discerning. This lack of perception on her part was attributable to the fact that the rounded frames of her glasses got in the way whenever Phoebe happened to be looking in a mirror. No one had ever been successful in talking Phoebe out of wearing the glasses, however. She felt they added an important professional touch to her business wardrobe.

Years from now—Phoebe told herself encouragingly as a huge black Labrador who had been sitting on the porch of the cabin gave a yelp and bounded forward— she would look back on this weekend as the most thrilling of her life. The thought was gratifying to the spirit of adventure and romance Phoebe usually tried to keep firmly under control but the practical side of her nature found it highly unfortunate that real adventure was composed of such a high degree of discomfort and fear.

The Lab trotted eagerly up to her and Phoebe leaned down to stroke his sleek head with a feeling of relief. The cheerful attitude of the advance greeting party gave her hope for an equally friendly welcome from the people in the cabin. Surely the owners of such a happy dog must be decent people. She gave a last pat to her new ally and then glanced up as the cabin door opened.

The man who lounged against the frame of the door regarded her without any of the dog's enthusiasm. In fact, he looked downright disgusted, Phoebe thought in surprise. Of course, it stood to reason that a man encountering a woman emerging from the forest at this hour might be hoping for something more in the line of delicate, svelte blonds rather than a brunette with a definite tendency toward *roundness*. But before she could open her mouth to begin what would only be an incredible explanation, her rescuing hero spoke.

"What the hell do you think you're doing? You can just turn right around and walk back to your car!"

It was too much. Phoebe was scratched, exhausted, hungry, and had barely survived a terrifying experience. She might not look like Venus rising from the waves but she certainly deserved better than this! Deliberately she pushed a lock of heavy, jungle cat brown hair which curved around her shoulders back behind an ear and glared at the man.

"I realize I'm probably not your type and I can assure you, you're not what I had hoped for either! Still, I need help and as you're the only one around, I'm going to have to impose on you. My name is Phoebe Hampton and I have just spent a miserable night in this forest, trying to follow the stream. Do you think you could bring yourself to spare me a cup of coffee and something to eat?" This last request contained a wistful note which Phoebe instantly regretted. But she really was very hungry. And tired. The black Lab, at least, responded to it with a concerned tongue which leaped out to caress her hand. The man, on the other hand, did not seem in the least impressed.

"If you're hungry, I imagine it's your own damn fault. You should have thought to pack some food in with you. Or didn't my charming aunt . . ." he broke off, leaving Phoebe wondering how his aunt had entered the conversation. "Where did you park your car?" he continued impatiently, moving a little further out on the porch and leaning forward to plant two strong, competent-looking hands against the railing. Doing so brought him fully into the sunlight and revealed the brilliant red of his hair and bushy brows. Ice blue eyes ran speculatively over her figure in blue jeans and plaid shirt and Phoebe abruptly wished she had stayed on that last diet. But she had gotten so tired of broiled grapefruit and poached eggs!

"I didn't drive," she explained politely, "I was driven. Somewhere up there." Phoebe waved a hand which indicated the vague distance behind her. "Oh, I had a car but it broke down last night on the highway. I was on my way to the coast, you see," she added helpfully. "I had rented the car for the weekend on one of those special rates the rental companies give and when it died, I was so furious that I got out and started walking. When these two creeps in a pickup came along and offered to help, I was stupid enough to think they were just a couple of nice farm boys . . ." Phoebe blinked back tears of frustration and fury. How could she have been so dumb? "They turned off the highway shortly after picking me up and . . . and just kept driving. It seemed like hours!" She took a steadying breath. "I was taken to a cabin and as the situation was deteriorating rapidly I thought I'd best take the first opportunity of getting myself free." Phoebe swallowed as a dark memory momentarily clouded her clear sea eyes. No doubt about it, she decided, real, genuine fear was not a pleasant aspect of adventuring.

She noticed the pure disbelief in the redheaded man's icy eyes. Damn! Why couldn't she have stumbled on someone with a more, well, heroic nature? A tall, dark, handsome soul who would have instantly detected the state she was in, taken one look into her eyes with his own dark, intense gaze, and known she was telling the truth? This man didn't appear to have a gallant bone in his body. For some reason, a part of her brain noted that the body in question wasn't too far off the proper heroic mold. True, he was only about five inches taller than Phoebe but the lean, strong lines of his build weren't softened at all by spare flesh. The observation was somewhat forced on her due to the fact that the man was dressed only in close fitting, faded jeans. A bare chest covered with curling red hairs tapered into a flat, hard stomach which paired with narrow hips. The proportions were fine, she admitted to herself. A couple of inches more height, black hair with steel grey eyes, and he would have been perfect. Well, in her situation she would just have to be grateful for whatever she got. It was obvious she wasn't his idea of perfection, either! But things could have been worse. The main job now was to convince him she needed help.

"I'm sure your fellow conspirator, Aunt Flo, has already told you I don't have a telephone up here. The absence of phones and electricity is one of the main attractions of the place," the man told her ruthlessly. "Which means, of course, there's no way to verify your story short of driving back down the mountain which I do not intend to do until Monday morning!"

"But this is only Saturday!" Phoebe observed, surprised by this latest twist. The police should be notified as soon as possible, she knew.

"Correct. I am suitably impressed by your powers of observation but the innocently astonished look is somewhat overdone. Aunt Flo should have briefed you more thoroughly. Now suppose you tell me the truth and then hike back out to where you parked your car? You can report the failure to my aunt and that will be the end of the matter. I'm feeling reasonably tolerant this time."

"Tolerant?" Phoebe inquired cautiously, trying to grasp just who he appeared to think she was. Or had she stumbled onto a madman?

"I'm afraid I lost my temper the last time my aunt tried her matchmaking techniques. The girl wound up in tears and Flo didn't speak to me for a month. Now, unless you want to bring things to the same conclusion this time, I suggest you leave at once. Jinx! Come here!" he called to the dog who had taken up residence at Phoebe's feet. The black Lab glanced at him soulfully and remained where he was.

"Thanks for the vote of confidence, friend!" Phoebe smiled down at the dog who thumped his tail in return. "You'd give me a cup of coffee, wouldn't you?"

9

"That dog usually displays more common sense!" The man shrugged one shoulder disgustedly and turned to go back inside the cabin, calling back to her, "The hell with it! Come on in and I'll give you a cup before I send you packing!" Muttering something about being too damn softhearted, he vanished into the dark interior.

Phoebe hesitated a moment, her nimble mind logging the harsh, arrogant planes of her host's face, the cool blue eyes, and the forbidding tone of his voice. Not a particularly warm welcome, all in all. She was going to have her work cut out for her, she decided, convincing him first not to force her back into the woods and second that she needed a ride down the mountain to the nearest police station or sheriff's office. But, then wasn't she accustomed to handling men and getting what she wanted from them? At least, she admonished herself sadly, she was usually successful in the business world. The same could not honestly be said about her private life. Well, she would view this as a difficult business arrangement and take it from there. Straightening tired shoulders, Phoebe hurried forward with the dog at her heels. For a cup of hot coffee she felt she could tolerate a few insults. She had to get a foot in the door somewhere.

She climbed the two shaky steps onto the porch and peered into the cabin doorway. There was only one room. Windows set in the wooden walls let in a certain amount of sunlight which, in turn, illuminated the wooden floor with its treadbare rug in front of a stone fireplace. An old Salvation Army relic of a chair was placed to take advantage of the hearth on which was stacked a hefty pile of kindling and logs. A cot with a sleeping bag rolled neatly at the end occupied a side wall and a small wood stove completed the furnishings except for a few odds and ends which Phoebe didn't have time to examine. Definitely a bachelor retreat, she thought, moving toward the stove where the redheaded man was pouring out the coffee she would, at that moment, cheerfully have fought for. A pan of water resting on a table caught her eye.

"Do you mind if I wash my hands first?" she inquired politely. Taking his brusque nod as an invitation to proceed she quickly scrubbed her hands and dried them on a nearby dish towel—which was none too clean, she noticed. Well, with any luck, a commodity which she had not been favored with lately, the hand-washing would get rid of the some of the poison oak toxins.

"Thank you," Phoebe murmured with great feeling, reaching out to wrap her fingers around the chipped mug being handed to her. Long lashes dipped behind the dusty lenses of her glasses as she closed her eyes to inhale the aroma appreciatively. When she glanced up again it was to find the man perched on the table, studying her with a mixture of curiosity and wariness. Standing so close to him she was suddenly very aware of the naked, nicely tanned chest. No, the muscles didn't ripple and bulge across his shoulders, but there was a sensation of wiry strength in him which she couldn't help comparing with Richard. He wasn't as tall as Richard, who towered over her in the best romantic tradition. And, of course, he didn't have Richard's marvelous black hair and silvery-grey eyes, but there was something about this man . . .

"It got rather cold last night. Good thing you knew enough not to asphyxiate yourself by running the car heater too much while you waited to make your grand entrance," her host said heartlessly. "Come on, you can

11

drink the coffee out on the porch. There's a table and a couple of chairs out there." Pouring himself a cup, he led the way toward the door. Phoebe followed obediently, cradling the mug carefully and casting longing glances at the ice chest standing in the corner.

"I know this sounds picky but do you have any canned milk?" she asked after taking an experimental sip of the thick brew.

"There's some in the cupboard over the stove," he told her grudgingly. He went on out to the porch and sat down somewhere just beyond her range of vision. Phoebe thought quickly. If she moved fast enough . . .

"I'll get it and be right out!" she called, moving purposefully toward the ice chest.

Inside lay a wealth of temptation. A carton of eggs, a package of bacon, bread, and much more were nestled there. It was too much. Phoebe told herself she was not going to starve in the midst of plenty simply because she had been unlucky enough to find an ungallant, ungracious hero!

"Have you had breakfast yet?" she raised her voice to inquire, hunting through a small cupboard for a frying pan.

"No, I'll eat after you're on your way," he yelled back firmly.

"You're going to have a long wait, pal," Phoebe whispered as she set about the business of preparing breakfast with her usual casual efficiency. Jinx sat watching expectantly.

"What's going on in here?" a harsh voice demanded a few minutes later and Phoebe glanced up to see the man's sleek shoulders blocking off the light in the doorway. The smell of frying bacon drifted tantalizingly across the room and out of the corner of her eye she saw his nose twitch in response.

"I'm not accustomed to wood stoves, but you seem to

have a healthy fire going in there," Phoebe motioned to the potbellied iron stove. "And it looks as if you've got more than enough food to see you through until Monday so I decided to help myself. Out of the goodness of my heart," she concluded sweetly, "I decided to cook enough for two."

"The hell you did! Now listen to me, woman . . ."

"Phoebe. Phoebe Hampton," she corrected him idly, turning bacon with a fork. "I didn't catch your name?"

"That's because you know damn well what it is!" he thundered, regarding the delicious smelling breakfast with a curious combination of hunger and frustration.

The way to a man's heart, Phoebe thought grimly. When you couldn't knock 'em over with seductive green eyes, blond hair, and a delicate, sexy figure, you resorted to the practical approach. Feeding men well always seemed to put them in a better mood, she had learned.

"The only thing I know about you at this point is that you've got a scheming aunt and you are blessed with a typical male ego," Phoebe informed him, sipping her coffee and eyeing the bacon with a critical eye. Any time now she should be able to pop the eggs into the frying pan.

"Is that right? And what's wrong with my ego?" he demanded. "Just because I'm onto my aunt's crazy schemes to compromise me with a woman, doesn't mean I've got an abnormally inflated ego!"

"I didn't say it was abnormally inflated. Merely that it was typical of the male of the species. They're all inflated. Ask any woman!" Phoebe smiled at him condescendingly and slid the eggs neatly into the pan. Before he could comment further she said blithely, "But tell me more about this compromising business. I'll admit it has a lovely, romantic ring to it, but it just doesn't happen in this day and age!"

13

"I didn't say I would consider myself compromised," he replied vengefully, "only that my Aunt Flo thinks somehow she can force me to the altar that way. My poor aunt lives in a different world part of the time, if you haven't already guessed."

"A world in which a man might still feel duty-bound to do the honorable thing?" Phoebe grinned, poking gently at an egg.

"Exactly. Comes from reading too many of those historical romances!"

Phoebe winced, thinking of the shelf full of such romances she had at home.

"On her previous attempts, she's usually involved unsuspecting, helpless little types who might really be hurt. I'll have to admit you're outside the normal style!"

"Ah!" Phoebe announced with dawning comprehension as she flipped bread over on the griddle and soaked it in real butter. None of the low cholesteral stuff for this man, she noted. "I see. I was supposed to be a misty-eyed little femme fatale! Well, I've always wanted to be, at least for a weekend. But one of the hard facts of life is that you're stuck with the hard facts of life. I'm dreadfully sorry to be such a disappointment but when you get back to . . . ?" She glanced at him inquiringly, "Portland?" At his grudging nod she continued. "When you get back there, you'll probably find the next candidate waiting in line, fragile and blond. Where does your aunt dig them up, I wonder?"

"The last one was a daughter of one of her bridge partners! The one before that was the niece of one of the members of her garden club! Where the hell did she find you, anyway?" He sounded genuinely interested. She must be markedly different from the norm, Phoebe thought with an inner grimace.

"Perhaps she decided it was time to switch to a new

style for you. Poor man! What your life must be like! Even in this day and age it would take a firm resolve to go around seducing the relatives of your aunt's best friends and then refusing to marry them! I mean, the daughter of a bridge partner!''

"I didn't seduce them!" He snapped in a very irritated tone. "The type of female my aunt sees fit to pester me with is not the type I care for!"

"I see," Phoebe nodded wisely. "You don't like fragile blonds. Perhaps you prefer redheads? You like looking like a matched set of dolls when you go out?"

"Oh, I like fragile blonds," he shot back, a gleam entering the piercing blue eyes momentarily. "It's just that I prefer them a bit older and wiser than what Aunt Flo usually locates! Someone more your age, for example!"

"One who won't go crying to Aunt Flo and her mother when the affair is over?"

"Exactly!"

"Let's eat," Phoebe instructed firmly, dishing out the meal and handing him a plate which he accepted with a look of surprise. Picking up some knives and forks she led the way out onto the porch with the same confident manner she would have handled a room full of upper management.

"How old are you, precisely?" the annoying man asked as he followed her. "Twenty-six? Twenty-seven?"

"Twenty-seven," she informed him aloofly, seating herself. "Old enough, as you say, to know better than to think a man like you would marry me to make an honest woman out of me!"

"Ouch! I think my aunt has a better opinion of my honor than you do!" he groaned with a hint of a smile as he lowered his lean frame onto the chair beside her and hoisted a fork.

15

"I'm starving!" Phoebe noted fervently, munching a piece of toast with delicate greed. Privately she was thinking that her companion must be around thirty-four or thirty-five. And he looked as if he'd lived every year of that estimate! Small crinkles at the corners of the blue eyes and laugh lines around the hard shape of his mouth gave evidence that he could enjoy the world at the same time that he challenged it.

"You do look a little on the undernourished side," he remarked with what Phoebe felt to be unnecessary snideness.

"Used to the skinny types, hmmm?" she smiled back sunnily, digging into her food with a passion engendered as much by a strange sense of hurt as by hunger. If he were a gentleman he would not have called attention to her figure. Before he could get in another such comment she went on quickly,

"Look, I realize you don't believe me but I truly don't know your name and it's difficult cooking breakfast for a man under such circumstances. Could you humor me?"

"I'm Harlan Garand, as if you weren't very well aware," he said becoming a trifle more accommodating as he ate. It was understandable that a man might be a bit testy before breakfast, Phoebe decided. She had been right to feed him.

"Thank you. And what do you do for a living? I mean, when you're not running from teenage beauty queens?"

"I'm sure my aunt has filled you in on all the details!" he said unhelpfully.

Phoebe tried again. "Well, actually we were rather in a hurry and there were some vague areas . . ."

"What do you imagine I do?" he asked sarcastically. The mouth full of egg blunted the tone somewhat, however, and the blue eyes regarded her with a certain curiosity as if wondering how far she was prepared to carry the story.

Phoebe leaned back in her chair and studied him. It was necessary to keep some sort of conversation going she realized. If she talked long enough she might be able to convince him of her plight. He really ought to put on a shirt she thought absently. So much masculine flesh on display at this hour was disconcerting. However, it did give her a starting point. Feeling as if she deserved a spot of revenge for his comment on her own figure, she coolly allowed her gaze to travel the lean hard length of him.

"Perhaps you're an artist? One of those terribly intense creatures who ignore food while they're working?" Smiling benignly at his startled expression she continued enthusiastically. "Yes, a lean, hungry, artistic type whose dear aunt is worrying herself sick, wondering what will become of you if she doesn't find you a nice girl to settle down with. After all, you aren't getting any younger . . ." She broke off deliberately to survey the touches of grey barely noticeable at his temples and then went on. "Or maybe you're an airport control tower operator who sits hunched over a radar screen all day long, drinking tons of coffee, and living on tension and nerves. Then again you might be a tennis bum; traveling the world with the beautiful people and living on junk food. Yes, that might be it. Wasting your life away until your poor aunt has decided to make a last ditch effort to force you into a more conventional life style before you burn yourself out . . ."

"I do not," Harlan Garand announced wrathfully, "play tennis! Nor do I work in a control tower and I have never painted a stroke in my life since kindergarten! I get the point. It's obvious you find my masculine physique somewhat on the thin side but don't think that means I'm susceptible to a mothering

17

approach! As it happens, I have a perfectly healthy appetite and I am quite capable of cooking for myself, as Aunt Flo is well aware. If her latest tactic is to fix me up with a little domestic type, she's way off base!''

He paused, gathering a deep, indignant breath. ''Furthermore, it might interest you to know I am not considered unattractive by all members of the opposite sex.''

Phoebe smiled kindly, sensing herself on safe territory suddenly. True, his tone of voice was rather intimidating, but she had pursued enough business strategies in high tension situations to know that the eyes were where the truth resided. And there was a definite gleam now in that blue gaze, even though the brows above it were bunched ferociously.

''Perhaps some of the scrawnier members of the female community might find you appealing, but . . .'' Phoebe moved one hand in a languid, dismissing gesture as she let her words tail off meaningfully.

For an instant she wasn't altogether certain she had judged her man correctly. Just for a second she wondered if she had misread that flicker in the icy eyes and then Harlan gave a crack of appreciative laughter. It was, Phoebe decided, a pleasant sound and she grinned in response.

''All right,'' he finally chuckled, ''We're even! Do you always get revenge?''

''You know what they say,'' Phoebe grinned, ''don't get mad; get even!'' She paused and then asked interestedly, ''Tell me, why is your aunt so determined to marry you off?''

Harlan shrugged. ''Didn't she tell you her fears about me never marrying and providing her with lots of grandchildren to spoil?'' When Phoebe shook her head, he continued. ''Well, after my mother died, Aunt Flo cared for me. She never married and I played a very important role in her life, I guess—the family she never had. As a result she's every bit as concerned about my future as a real mother would be. Perhaps more so."

"You do return her affection, don't you?"

"I love Aunt Flo dearly. But she's not going to dictate my love life!"

Phoebe nodded understandingly. "I know exactly how you feel!"

"You do?" This was said with a fair degree of skepticism.

Phoebe nodded vigorously. "Absolutely. I have a brother who went so far as to actually try and buy me a husband!"

Harlan stared. "What happened?" He appeared fascinated in spite of himself.

"Well, you have to understand that after our parents died, Steven and I naturally grew very close. He's a real brain, you know. Invents things. The royalties started coming in while he was in his early twenties. He's well into his second million, as far as I know. At any rate, he thought I should have the kind of man I've always dreamed of. Tall, dark and handsome. Steve also thought he should be from a good family, if you know what I mean. We had been born into ye olde middle class and he decided I should practice a little upward mobility."

Phoebe moved her hands expressively. "Well, he picked out a good candidate from among his friends on the golf course, brought him home, and I promptly fell head over heels in love. I was twenty-five at the time," she added, wanting to explain her poor judgment.

"Go on," Harlan prompted. She couldn't tell whether or not he believed a word of what she was saying, but at least he didn't stop the conversation.

"That's about it. I had a whirlwind courtship and the next thing I knew found myself engaged. Unfor-

19

tunately, three weeks before the wedding I discovered the real reason my tall, dark, and handsome fiance had done such an enthusiastic job of sweeping me off my feet!'' Phoebe's blue-green eyes clouded. ''Steve had paid off his family's debts and gotten them back on their feet.''

''A touching story,'' Harlan said mockingly.

''Better than the one you told me!'' she pointed out spiritedly.

''Mine has the virtue of being true!''

''So is mine!''

''It's strange. With eyes like yours, I would have thought you would have had a very difficult time lying successfully,'' Harlan commented.

Abruptly Phoebe's lower lip threatened to tremble. She was so tired and this man was so obstinate. Unconsciously she rubbed the bridge of her nose in a little gesture of fatigue, closing her eyes to try to think of how best to approach him.

''Please, couldn't you bring yourself to at least let me stay here with you if you won't drive me down the mountain? I really don't have a car parked conveniently down the road. I wouldn't even know how to find the main highway from here! And it would be a very long walk out of these woods, even if I followed the trail, which I'm afraid to do. They might be looking for me.''

''Who might be looking for you?'' he pounced, obviously hoping to trap her.

''Those two punks who grabbed me yesterday,'' she said wearily. ''I feel safe here with you and, although I think I'd survive another night on this mountain, I don't like the prospect at all!'' It was true, she thought dimly, she did feel safe here. In spite of his ungentlemanly behavior there was a compelling aura of strength around this man. The added sense of protection provided by his large dog was not lost on Phoebe either.

No, if he wouldn't drive her to the police, she had to make him let her stay until he was ready to leave on Monday morning. She couldn't face the thought of making her way down to civilization alone!

"You're going to stick by that crazy tale?" Harlan demanded irritably.

"I haven't got a better one and I'm too exhausted to think one up at the moment," Phoebe smiled apologetically.

He sighed. "I meant what I said, you know. I'm not leaving until the weekend is over." A frown knitted the heavy brows.

"I know. I can wait. Probably no one's even missed me yet. Ferd will start getting upset this evening. I told him I intended to be back Saturday night. And I told Richard I would see him Sunday night so he's not like to come around until then. He won't really start to worry until Monday morning. I didn't have any other plans involving friends this weekend so no one's going to wonder about me. It's a shame to let the trail of those two punks get so cold, though. But maybe the police won't believe my story, either," she added, struck by the thought. Surely what the men in the truck had done constituted kidnapping and there would have been a rape charge involved if she hadn't freed herself when she did, but how would she ever prove it?

"It's not likely they'll listen to your tale if I'm the one who brings you back to Portland on Monday morning," Harlan agreed drily. "Who's Ferd?"

"An evil-tempered budgerigar who shares my apartment with me. Parakeet to you," Phoebe smiled wanly. "I got him on sale."

"Ferd the Bird?" A hint of a smile touched the hard mouth for an instant.

Phoebe nodded, thinking of how upset Ferd was going to be at having been left alone for the entire weekend. Luckily she had filled his seed and water dishes Friday morning. He wouldn't starve to death.

"And Richard?" Harlan pushed almost gently.

"You'll let me stay?" Phoebe asked eagerly, sensing that he was weakening.

"I didn't say that," he corrected quickly. "I intended to spend the weekend alone, without any females in the neighborhood. All I wanted to do was fish and maybe hike a bit. You're spoiling everything with this stupid trick. What did you do? Get someone to drop you off down at the main road and then hike in here so you would have the excuse of not having a car to take yourself back to Portland? And who is Richard, anyway?"

Phoebe sighed. "Richard is Richard Elton Chambers III. Sometimes known as merely the Third to me and my off-base sense of humor. You're the only one who knows that, by the way. I've always been careful to refer to him as Richard. Never Dick, of course." she added absently.

"Of course," Harlan nodded seriously and then glanced down at the dishes on the table in front of him. But not before Phoebe had seen the spark of humor moving deep in the blue eyes. "Are you going to offer to repay breakfast by washing the dishes?" he inquired, glancing up again.

"Some people would consider that having cooked it was sufficient payment," Phoebe noted.

"I'm feeling a little put upon at the moment," he retorted. "I think you ought to offer to wash them, too."

"Ah, well. No such thing as a free lunch, I suppose," Phoebe replied with what she privately considered a rather good-natured tone of voice. She was so tired! "Down at the stream, I take it?" she asked, getting painfully to her feet and stacking the plates and mugs.

Harlan nodded, watching her curiously, a ghost of a

smile touching the corners of his firm mouth. "Sorry. No running water, either. Didn't my aunt brief you?" For some reason he followed her down to the bank, propping himself against a rock to watch the process. There was a hint of approval in his eyes when she rinsed the dishes away from the flowing water but he said nothing.

"Why won't Richard the Third be checking up on you until Sunday night?" Harlan suddenly asked as Phoebe dried her water-numbed fingers on the towel. She looked at him, surprised by the reintroduction of Richard as a topic of conversation.

"Sunday night I'm supposed to have thought the whole matter over and perhaps changed my mind." Phoebe arranged herself as comfortably as possible against a sun-warmed boulder and leaned her head back tiredly. A slight rasping sound made her lift a hand to her thick hair only to find a leaf embedded in it. Hateful man! She thought grimly. He could have mentioned the fact earlier!

"Forgive me for sounding somewhat dense. But what exactly is Richard hoping to hear from you?"

"I told him I'd let him know whether or not I'd changed my mind about not marrying him," Phoebe explained, closing her eyes. Richard seemed very far away now, both geographically and in her thoughts. Last night had given her several hours in which to fulfill her promise and think about her decision. After the initial fear of being found by her kidnappers had faded, there hadn't been much else to think about except where to place her feet as she made her way downhill following the stream. She hadn't dared try and find the main road. That would have made it too easy for her captors. So, she had spent the long difficult hours thinking about Richard.

"Well? Did you?" Harlan asked. Then he spoiled the

human interest he was displaying by adding, "Or did you decide to wait and see how you made out with me, first?"

"Nope." Phoebe tried to summon up a little spirit. "I made up my mind before I even found your cabin! I'm going to give Richard the same answer that I gave him earlier. Of course, I will explain that I'm suitably aware of the honor he is offering and go on to say how I hope we can remain friends but that I just don't think we'd be very happy together."

"What will Richard say?" Harlan asked as if he couldn't resist.

Phoebe opened one eye to see him watching her intently. "He'll point out that I'm not getting any younger, that he can give me a very fashionable life style, that he's really very fond of me . . ."

"Merely fond?"

"You don't know Richard," Phoebe told him wisely, closing her eye again. "A blazing love is not quite his style. Such a pity, too. He certainly looks the part."

"What part?"

"You know, the tall, dark, handsome, masterful type. The kind women always break their hearts over. Or would if the type really existed outside of romantic novels." Phoebe wriggled a bit, settling herself more comfortably against the sun-warmed boulder. "But I imagine it's not altogether his fault. Richard was born with a position to uphold, you know."

"No, I didn't know. What position?" Humor was edging Harlan's voice again and Phoebe had the impression she was beginning to serve as a source of amusement for him. Well, it was one way of paying her way.

"The position of being the Third, naturally," she said clearly as if to a not-very-bright nine-year-old.

24

"Haven't you ever met any fine, upstanding types who come from fine, upstanding families with just the proper amount of fine, upstanding money?" Phoebe frowned questioningly, opening her eyes briefly to peer at him through the lenses of her glasses.

"You look quite fierce when you do that," Harlan commented apropos of nothing as far as she could tell.

"Do what?" she asked blankly, frowning still more.

"Frown like that behind those glasses."

"Oh." She shut her eyes again. So tired! And her muscles ached.

"To get back to your question," Harlan's voice went on smoothly. "Yes, I have met a few people such as you describe . . ." There was a distinct pause. "The name Chambers is beginning to ring a distant bell." There was another pause but Phoebe was too worn out to open her eyes to see his expression. "Are you trying to tell me you've decided you don't want the type of marriage Chambers is offering?"

"I'm one of those idiotic women who read too many romantic novels. Rather like your aunt, I guess," Phoebe explained, feeling herself succumbing rapidly to sleep. "We like to think that somewhere there is a tall, good-looking, wonderfully domineering man waiting to sweep us off our feet. Some women don't compromise. Your aunt may have been one. Personally, I'm giving myself three more years to find him. If he hasn't shown up by the time I'm thirty, I'll start looking at the Richard the Thirds of this world."

It was only as she felt herself going off completely that a stray thought flashed across her exhausted brain. She never had found out what Harlan Garand did for a living. She heard him move, heard him mutter something about how worn out she looked, and then she was asleep.

chapter two

When Phoebe awoke some time later it was to the combined prodding of a damp, inquisitive nose and a bracingly masculine voice. She was pleased with the level of alertness that allowed her to distinguish the fact that the nose and the voice each had different owners.

"Lunch time. Going to sleep all day?" said the voice, obviously not intending to let her have the luxury of going back to sleep even if she answered the question in the affirmative.

Phoebe opened her eyes, groped automatically for her glasses, and sat up as she pushed the frames in place. Funny, she didn't remember removing them but she must have because they were conveniently at hand beside her. The dog, who owned the wet nose, whined happily and licked her cheek affectionately. Somebody is glad to have me here, Phoebe thought, feeling pleased. She stroked the black fur and looked up at Harland Garand, wondering if he'd made up his mind about letting her stay the weekend.

"Are you waiting lunch for me?" she asked naively blinking in the light of a sun which had reached its zenith and wondering if she dared ask the other, more crucial question.

"Not exactly," he explained kindly, stretching down a hand to help her rise. The other hand held fishing tackle and a basket. "I'm waiting for you to fix my lunch."

26

"I see." She peered toward the basket. "Fresh fish for me to fry?"

"Don't get sassy."

"That means you didn't have any luck," Phoebe smiled sympathetically.

"Right. So you're going to have to throw something together out of the ice chest. I wasn't in the proper frame of mind for good fishing," he added by way of excuse. "I have reached a decision, however. I can't figure out a way to make sure you get safely back to Portland if you really haven't got a car—not without ruining my entire weekend by driving you back. So you can stay. But if you're going to enjoy the accommodations, you can damn well pay the tab!"

Relief washed over Phoebe, reflecting itself in her blue-green eyes. His own narrowed in response. He was going to let her stay, she thought exultantly. This notion was immediately followed by a small cautionary voice.

"You mean I'll pay my way by doing the cooking and the dishwashing?" she hazarded, wanting to make certain they each understood the other.

"Are you volunteering any other services?" he countered, cocking one red brow.

"Not if it means digging a new pit for the outhouse!" she grinned.

"How about if it means warming my sleeping bag?" he asked interestedly, blue eyes glinting in the clear sunlight.

Phoebe flushed but pulled herself together quickly. He was only teasing her, of course. She manufactured a sigh of mock regret and fixed him with her most mournful expression.

"Isn't it a pity I'm not your type? Don't fret, though, I really am a pretty good cook!"

"A man alone in the wilderness can make certain

27

adjustments," he pointed out. "It's true, I normally prefer the willowy blond types, but it gets awfully chilly around here when the sun goes down. You look as if you might be nice and . . . cuddly." Phoebe glimpsed the laughter in his eyes and refused to be intimidated. Yes, she could manage this man. He wasn't any different from most males. And she sensed no viciousness in him. She would be in no more danger of sharing his bed than she wished to be!

"I'm refusing for your own good, you know," she confided. "Think of how you'll be able to face your aunt with a clear conscience knowing you didn't actually seduce me. Besides, think of me! Do I deserve to be ravished, only to be abandoned, a shattered husk of a woman, after we return to Portland and you go back to willowy blonds?" Phoebe was strugging to contain her laughter and failing badly. "I couldn't bear to have my heart so cruelly broken!" She turned and started back toward the cabin, still chuckling. Jinx danced happily at her heels.

"You're absolutely right. I wouldn't want you to suffer from a broken heart caused by me, but I am considering the satisfaction of seeing you suffer from a well-tanned rear end!" Harlan announced, striding up the steps beside her and holding open the door of the cabin with unconscious courtesy. At least Phoebe assumed it was unconscious. After all, it wasn't as if she were a welcomed guest! She grinned back at him, assessing his lean build and the height which wasn't so much greater than her own. What was he? Five-foot-ten or so? She stood five-foot-five inches herself.

"You'd have to catch me first, and even then I think the battle would be fairly equal! Some of this, er, roundness of mine is muscle, you know!" she threatened lightly.

His blue eyes glinted again. "Better keep in mind that you're still here only because I can't figure out a way to get rid of you! I expect a little more in the way of groveling appreciation."

"I'll remember," Phoebe promised, running a hand through her tangled hair and watching as another leaf fell from it. "I haven't had much experience groveling, you understand, though."

"I'll be happy to instruct you," Harlan announced taking a menacing step forward, eyes alight with devilment.

"Perhaps after lunch?" she suggested, stepping backward quickly and holding out a hand placatingly. They might not be each other's preferred romantic types, she knew, but it was still better to keep things on a superficial, bantering level. Just to be on the safe side, physical contact should be avoided, Phoebe told herself, assessing the situation with all the skill she normally applied to managing her department at the large timber firm where she worked. She wasn't altogether certain about why he had changed his mind about letting her stay so quickly. She had been prepared for more discussion on the issue, but now that she'd won a partial victory, she didn't intend to lose control of the situation. Perhaps after lunch she might even reintroduce the idea of him driving her back to Portland. After all, if Harlan had given up the initial fight against letting her stay so readily . . .

"You think a bit of food will tame the savage beast again?" he inquired.

"I thought it might be worth a try. I'm really not yet in my best fighting form."

"I noticed you must have had a hard time of it walking in from the main road this morning. Why didn't you stick to the trail? You appear to have taken the scenic route!''

"I've told you, I didn't come from the main road. I followed the stream and there wasn't any trail!'' Phoebe responded briefly, turning away to sort through items in the ice chest. When she moved to the small table with her hands full of sandwich makings she noticed he had placed his fishing tackle neatly against the wall and was rummaging around in his overnight bag. An instant later he pulled out a shabby looking work shirt and slipped it on.

"It's going to be interesting to see if you stick by your kidnap story all weekend,'' he remarked, buttoning the shirt.

"Is that why you decided to let me stay? To see if you could browbeat the truth out of me?'' Phoebe asked sweetly, slicing tomatoes.

"Well, I have to admit this is definitely a new approach from Aunt Flo. If she wanted to whet my curiosity, she's done it this time. But, to be honest, the main factor in my decision was the fact that you're old enough to know better than to get involved in a situation like this. People might be able to make life difficult for me if I drove back to town Monday morning with a child just out of her teens . . .''

"But they'll just look at me and say I should have had more sense, right?''

"Right!'' He sauntered over to the frayed arm of the old chair in front of the fireplace and settled down on it, watching as she prepared the sandwiches. "And in the meantime, it might not be so unhandy to have a cook and housekeeper around the place. I mean, it's not as if you're a guest I'll have to entertain.''

"I'm glad you're beginning to look on the positive side,'' Phoebe muttered drily. "Do you want mustard on your sandwich?''

"Would I have packed mustard if I didn't like it?" he asked reasonably.

"Excellent point," she chuckled, spreading mustard liberally on both sandwiches. A more in-depth search of the ice chest produced a couple of apples and some cheese. "Good thing you packed a lot of food," she commented, putting the small repast together attractively on a platter and hoisting the whole thing expertly on one palm. Summers spent working as a waitress during her college years still paid occasional dividends, she reflected.

"It's your responsibility to ration the food through Monday morning," Harlan informed her, rising lazily to his feet. "Running out would really put me in a bad frame of mind."

"I trust I don't have to make it go three ways?" Phoebe asked, glancing at the tail-wagging Labrador who had levered himself to his feet to follow them out onto the porch.

"Jinx's food is in a sack in the closet," Harlan told her helpfully, sitting down at the small table and reaching greedily for one of the handfilling sandwiches.

Phoebe didn't reply but settled back in her chair to enjoy the meal. It was so peaceful here within sight of the stream. Hard to believe that only last night she had been so frightened and cold and hungry. Idly she slipped a piece of cheese to Jinx who had settled himself near her under the table. Would the two so-called hunters be out looking for her? They had started drinking shortly after picking her up. Perhaps they had sobered enough by this morning to decide the safest thing to do would be to hightail it out of the area? Phoebe tried to put herself in their place. A couple of guys out for a weekend in the woods, complete with rifles and beer, had spotted a woman alone and decided to have some "fun." But their victim had escaped and by now they must realize there was a chance she could provide enough descriptive evidence to help the police apprehend them if she chose to. True, many potential rape victims would not want to get involved with the law, but they couldn't know for certain how Phoebe would react. One of them, at least, would be harboring a grudge. Phoebe had thrown a pan full of boiling water in his face before making her escape. She shuddered involuntarily. She could still hear his outraged scream of pain.

"What are you thinking?" Harlan's voice broke into her thoughts, sounding genuinely curious. Phoebe swung her intelligent gaze to meet his.

"About last night."

"You don't look too pleased. Not working out as planned, huh? I imagine it's because this is one of those schemes which look a good deal better in the evening than they do in the cold light of day?" His lofty tones were laced with mock sympathy.

"Something like that," Phoebe agreed disinterestedly, too relaxed at the moment to work up any antagonism. That nap this morning had been precisely what she needed. How far had she walked last night? It had seemed safer to keep moving and she had allowed herself only one short rest period a couple of hours before dawn. But it had been so cold, rest had been impossible and after a short time she had pushed herself to her feet, knowing she had to get down the mountain. She wondered where she had read that advice about following a stream to find one's way off a mountain. Probably in one of the romantic adventures she read in such quantities. The thought made her smile slightly. They were good for something, after all, even if they did tend to fill one's fantasies with images of impossibly tall, masterful men who never seemed to exist in real life. But then, in all fairness, the fiery, spirited heroines probably didn't exist, either!

"Don't worry too much about it," Harlan said with sudden, surprising gentleness. It took Phoebe a moment to realize he was referring to the scheme he felt had been perpetrated on him. "I know how persuasive my aunt can be and I know how her mind works." He smiled at her. "I'm sure she made the whole thing sound quite reasonable. You seem like a sensible sort of woman, though. I'm rather amazed you let her talk you into it!"

Phoebe couldn't help herself. She burst out laughing, flinging up one hand as if to ward off his words. "Please don't talk to me about being sensible! It goes along with having wholesome looks and a secure job! I'm trying to enjoy the weekend!"

"I think you get a fair share of enjoyment out of life," Harlan noted, munching his apple and eyeing her thoughtfully. "You look like a basically happy sort of person. Is the Third a happy person, too?"

They were back to Richard again. Why was Harlan so interested?

"Yes, in his own way, I think he is," Phoebe answered quietly. "It's just that his way could never be mine. I know it's probably foolish of me, but I want more out of a romance than he can give me. And he needs a different sort of wife too."

"He's dull?"

"Terribly," she sighed.

"Why did you let matters get to the point where he was asking you to marry him?" Harlan asked, sounding disapproving.

Phoebe glanced at him quickly, wondering if he deserved an answer. Harlan Garand certainly had no right to judge her actions! Still, it was a point she had pondered herself.

"A good question," she told him at last. "I'm not

sure how things got as far as they did. I expect it was because it was a comfortable situation at first. I was new in town and Richard makes a very pleasant escort, except that he hasn't got much of a sense of humor. But there I go, being picky."

"That's right. You forget the man has a position," Harlan admonished, the laughter dancing briefly in his blue eyes.

"True. Add to that the fact that I read far too many romance novels and it's plain to see the affair was doomed from the beginning," Phoebe smiled self-deprecatingly.

"So when my aunt and your mother proposed last night's little plan, it sounded rather exciting?" Harlan suggested understandingly.

Phoebe laughed and shook her head ruefully. "No fair trying to trap me! I'm having a hard enough time as it is keeping my version of events straight!"

"Keeps the conversation from dragging," Harlan pointed out rather more good-naturedly than Phoebe would have expected in the circumstances. "What do you think Richard the Third will say when I deliver you on Monday morning?"

Phoebe shrugged unconcernedly. "He hasn't got the right to say anything. I've already told him we're through . . ." A sudden thought struck Phoebe's romantic side at that moment, however. "But it would be interesting to know what he would say if he realized I'd spent the weekend with another man . . ." Her voice trailed off distantly as she tried to conjure up a picture of Richard jealous.

"I know what I'd do if I were him," Harlan said with unexpected, soft menace.

"What?" she asked curiously, fixing him with a direct, inquisitive look.

"If I considered you my property I would probably

half kill the other man and make sure you were made fully aware of my feelings!" The words were spoken so softly and with so much certainty that Phoebe started. "You'd never stray again," he promised, blue eyes holding hers in a steel mesh.

"Good grief! You are a violent type, aren't you? I can assure you, the Third would never resort to such activity, though. It wouldn't be fitting for someone in his position, you see. A jealous rage would mean a *scene*. Richard doesn't get involved in *scenes*!" Phoebe gave a little gurgle of laughter at the thought. "Besides, I'm just not the type of woman men get that worked up over!" she concluded ruefully.

"You're supposed to be spending this weekend rethinking his offer of marriage, Phoebe. If Chambers is any kind of man, you're playing with fire," Harlan warned her harshly and then added on a rough note, "Do you sleep with him?"

"No!" Phoebe was too flabbergasted at the unexpected question to give it the setdown it merited. The man certainly had an unholy nerve prying into her private life like this! Just because he was willing to tolerate her presence for a couple of days didn't mean there weren't limits! Belatedly, but with a strong feeling of righteous anger she told him, "It's none of your business, but the relationship never progressed quite that far!"

"Then maybe he won't come after me with a gun," Harlan remarked, seeming to relax.

Phoebe stared. "You never had any need to worry," she . informed him tightly, unable to conceive that Harlan Garand had seriously begun to fear Richard Elton Chambers III.

"I don't think you know that much about men," he replied coolly.

"Perhaps not that much about your kind of man,"

35

she retorted scathingly. "Is that how they settle things where you come from?"

Harlan grinned. A sharkline grin. "I only know how to handle things in a similar situation. If I'd bedded you and asked you to marry me, I'd definitely consider you private property until matters between us were well and truly over. Perhaps longer! Certainly as long as you were 'rethinking' a proposal of marriage from me! I wouldn't tolerate lightly an incident like this weekend!"

Phoebe fought to control the breathless feeling which was building in her chest and cast about desperately for a way to bring the conversation back under her command. In a distant corner of her mind a tiny voice wondered what life would have been like if Richard had taken such an approach to women. But, then, if he had, she wouldn't have been one of the women he would have approached! Men like that preferred spirited, sensuous little blonds or redheads. Perhaps with alluring green eyes . . .

"But what if, like the Third, you had only asked me to marry you and hadn't quite got around to making love to me?" she managed to counter, wondering why in the world she was asking such an incredibly provocative question! It wasn't like her at all!

"I can't see myself conducting such a restrained courtship." Harlan smiled more pleasantly now. Obviously his own imagination was at work, Phoebe thought grimly. Visions of a petite blond were apparently dancing in his brain. "If I were in love, I would be making every effort to take full advantage of the situation!"

Phoebe took a deep, steadying breath. "Well, all I can say is, you and Richard are two entirely different types of men and I may have been hasty in my initial decision to tell him I wouldn't marry him! He's beginning to seem quite civilized!"

"And dull," Harlan reminded her.

"And dull," Phoebe agreed with resignation. "Still, a woman should consider the positive side of the matter, as Richard has not been at a loss to point out. I'm not likely at this advanced age to encounter a man who will become more impassioned about me and Richard *is* fond of me. If I could excite him to a slightly higher degree of feeling . . . you've given me an idea." Phoebe drifted into silence, soft eyes focusing somewhere in the middle distance while she considered the situation.

"What's the idea?" Harlan demanded with a foreboding expression. The red brows laced together threateningly.

"Maybe I should try inciting a bit of jealousy in Richard. If you're right and even a mild-tempered man would become upset over an escapade like this weekend . . . perhaps there are hidden depths to his nature that I'm not yet aware of although I strongly doubt it . . ."

"Phoebe, I don't like the way your mind is working at the moment. If you're seriously interested in the man, which doesn't appear likely from what you've said, I suggest you go down on your hands and knees and beg his forgiveness for the mess you've gotten yourself into! The last thing you should be worrying about is making him jealous! Why do women always want to play that stupid game? If you want him, go back to Portland, tell him you got involved in this crazy scheme solely to make him jealous, that nothing really happened between you and the other man, and you're desperately sorry . . ." Harlan bit off the end of the sentence, apparently having trouble picturing Phoebe in such a dramatic role. She didn't blame him, it was a bit hard to imagine herself on her knees in front of Richard. "Maybe, just maybe, he'll let you off lightly!" Harlan concluded.

"Would you in his spot?" Phoebe asked shrewdly, the rational, practical side of her nature wondering why in the world she was being driven to continue this strange conversation with a man she had known less than a day!

"I might trust you if I loved you and believed that nothing had happened but I sure as hell wouldn't let you off very lightly. I'd take into consideration the fact that you'd done it on a foolish whim to make me jealous and proceed to give you a demonstration of what jealousy really is in a man! I'd want to make the point quite clear, you see, so you wouldn't be tempted to try it again!" Harlan quirked an eyebrow and met Phoebe's fascinated gaze with a level one of his own.

"Do you have a serious girlfriend?" she demanded breathlessly, sea eyes shining behind the lenses of her glasses as she contemplated him.

"I beg your pardon?" Harlan appeared a trifle nonplused at the switch in topics.

"Do you have a girlfriend? I mean, one you really care about?" she persisted.

"There is no one floating around at the moment to whom I plan to propose marriage, which is what I think you have in mind," he told her drily, eyes resting on her in a puzzled fashion. "Why?"

"Because you talk exactly like one of those marvelously domineering heroes in a romantic novel—the kind your aunt and I read. And I simply wondered if there was a woman in your life who was the recipient of all that masculine possessiveness and masterfulness," Phoebe explained impatiently, so well acquainted with the characteristics of such heroes that she forgot they might be unknown to her host.

"Are you planning to apply for the position?" he inquired politely, the blue gaze mirroring a combination of masculine confusion, humor, and a spark of indignation. He probably didn't appreciate the notion that he sounded like some character out of a novel, Phoebe decided with an inner grin.

"Good heavens, no!" she assured him honestly. "I'm well aware that neither of us is the other's ideal mate! But even if I were to find your characteristics in a tall, powerful type who could literally sweep me off my feet, I'd probably chicken out. All I'm asking is for someone whose temperament falls somewhere between Richard and yourself. A man with enough passion to be a bit possessive, but definitely not someone of whom I would have to be afraid. That would take all the fun out of the thing," she explained helpfully.

"I see. You think that any woman of mine would go in fear of me?" Harlan asked, obviously making a valiant effort to work through her obscure thinking.

"A woman with my nature and the physical characteristics of a petite blond—if that's not a contradiction in terms—would." Phoebe laughed. "You certainly do appear to have a violent sreak in you that would require a brave and spirited woman to handle."

"You don't consider yourself brave and spirited?" Harlan asked deliberately.

Phoebe smiled, her soft eyes brimming with humor. She shook her head in a negative gesture. "Oh, no. Not in the least. At my size and age and in my work bravery and spirit aren't the qualities a woman cultivates, even if she thought she had the rudiments of them!"

"I see. What qualities do you cultivate?" Harlan asked, looking intrigued.

"Practicality," Phoebe told him firmly. "Efficiency, a cost-effective approach to business matters, and practicality. Also cooking."

"How does the cooking fit in with those other fine qualities?" Harlan demanded, grinning.

"Cooking is what I hope to use to capture my man when I finally do meet him," she informed him wisely and deemed it time to terminate this incredible conversation. "Would you mind if I took a bath?" she asked abruptly, rising to her feet and collecting the remains of lunch.

"You do have a way of changing the subject," Harlan remarked, not bothering to assist her. Instead he stretched his legs out in front of him and fondled Jinx's ears with absent affection.

"Comes from years of practice ending lengthy business meetings," she told him, moving toward the door to the cabin. "What about the bath?"

"Well, you can use the stream. It's warmed up a bit now. Still going to be cold, though. There's some soap on the small table beside the cot. Be sure to rinse off away from the water, though!"

"Spoken like a true, environmentally conscious Oregonian," Phoebe tossed back over her shoulder.

"You ex-Californians are just jealous," Harlan chuckled.

"How did you know I'm from California?" she called back, hunting for the soap near the cot.

"We Oregonians can spot 'em a mile away."

The afternoon passed very comfortably or at least, Phoebe thought, it became comfortable when she had finally warmed her body back to a normal temperature after bathing in the chilled mountain stream. Harlan returned to his fishing, well above the spot Phoebe had chosen for bathing. Locating a worn paperback copy of a science fiction thriller, Phoebe settled down beside Jinx who was reclining near Harlan in the classic pose of the contented dog. There was little conversation between the three but a sense of companionship crept quietly into the atmosphere and lingered. Phoebe glanced up at one point to watch Harlan land the first fish of the day and realized with a start that she hadn't even thought about the unfortunate events of the preceding night for at least an hour.

"Congratulations!" she called obligingly when Harlan held the flapping fish for approval. "Who's going to clean it?"

"I'm including that among the household chores," he informed her, a warning gleam lighting the blue gaze. He placed his catch carefully into the basket. "You remember. The ones you're doing as a means of paying for the weekend!"

"The last fish I cleaned was in high school biology and that was intended to be a dissection! No telling what would remain of your poor fish if I actually attempted to clean it!" Phoebe thought it unnecessary to add that the biology exercise had nearly made her physically ill.

"I'll teach you," he told her and went back to his fishing. Phoebe lifted one brow aloofly and returned to her book. She had no intention of being coerced into cleaning Harlan's fish. Cook them, yes. Clean them, no.

Two hours later Harlan announced there was a sufficient quantity of fish for the evening meal and began to pack the tackle. The reel safely stowed into the box along with the rest of the gear, he reached in and removed a large, efficient-looking knife.

"Here you go," he informed Phoebe, handing it to her hilt first.

Phoebe's large eyes widened slightly behind the lenses of the tortoiseshell frames as she stared first at the knife and then at the man holding it out to her. He had meant what he said!

"Harlan, I'm not going to clean those fish!" she announced with absolute finality. "It would make me sick!"

"Are you hungry?" he asked simply, ice eyes glittering in the late afternoon sunlight.

"Yes, but . . ."

"Then you can clean them."

"I don't know how!" she tried plaintively. Phoebe decided that for the sake of harmony she would prefer to avoid a direct challenge. Perhaps he would back down if she pleaded ignorance. He couldn't force her to clean them, of course, but she wanted his good will for the remainder of the weekend. Still, nothing could make her clean those slippery looking fish!

"I told you I would teach you." Harlan reached into the basket and pulled out one of the creatures. Before Phoebe could look away he had removed the head with a neat slice and proceeded to finish the job.

Jinx observed the operation with mild interest and Phoebe watched in sick fascination. In a couple of minutes Harlan passed the bloodied knife into her unresisting palm and pulled another fish out of the basket.

Desperately she turned the full force of a pleading, almost green gaze on him, unaware herself just how potent it was. He seemed proof against it, however, and directed her firmly to get to work. The fish lay poised on a rock in front of her and he guided the hand holding the knife to the proper position.

"No!" Phoebe snapped out the refusal, recovering from the sight of the first opeation rapidly and getting a firm grip on herself. Anyone who knew her well would have recognized the uncompromising nature of her present tone. Many a man had backed down when she spoke in that voice in her work environment. It was cold, clear, and utterly final. Why, she wondered frantically, didn't Harlan seem to recognize it?

"Clean the fish, Phoebe, or so help me I'll do it with your hands under mine!" One hard, square hand reached out to close over hers as she held the knife limply in front of her. Deliberately he applied pressure and the blade began to sink into the scales squishily.

"It goes much more neatly if you do it with a quick, sharp blow," he told her grimly. "But we can saw our

42

way through if you prefer."

"*No*," Phoebe repeated, disgusted at the panicked note which had found its way into her voice. "Please, Harlan . . ." Even as she begged him to release her hand she exerted her own not inconsiderable strength in an effort to free it. It didn't budge him. This was ridiculous, she thought lightheadedly. She surely ought to be able to handle a situation like this! But she couldn't manage to free herself and the blade sank steadily downward. For a long instant there was a sharp, intense, silent battle of wills and muscles, and then an awful crunch came from the head of the fish. It was the last straw. Phoebe surrendered.

"All right, Harlan. I'll do it! I promise! But please stop this ghastly sawing business. I can't stand it!" It was true, she could feel her stomach beginning to churn. Anything would be better than this slow butchering!

Harlan released her immediately, holding her stunned eyes with his own.

"Don't ever get the idea," he told her coolly, "that simply because you convinced me to let you stay the weekend, you can manage me! When I feel strongly enough about an issue, I always win. Now clean the fish!"

Without a word, Phoebe lowered her smoldering gaze to the fish, swung the knife in a short, violent arc, and began the process of getting dinner on the table. A cook, she reminded herself, shouldn't balk at this end of the business. It was only because she had been lucky enough to be born into an age of supermarkets that she hadn't had to learn the task earlier. With bracing thoughts such as these and by pretending that each thrust of the knife was somehow a way of working out her anger at Harlan, she made it through the basket of fish.

"Maybe next time you'll think twice about crashing a

43

man's fishing weekend," was the only comment Harlan made when the job was done.

Phoebe said nothing, but got shakily to her feet and walked over to the stream to thoroughly wash her hands. Thank God, she wasn't going to lose control over her stomach! After the first two fish it had elected to settle down, a fact for which she was exceedingly grateful.

"Was that why you made me do it?" she asked without looking at him. Her words were remarkably calm and cool now. Harlan couldn't know it but it was a tone she generally reserved for making difficult members of corporate upper management see the errors of their ways. An aloof, superior tone which said clearly she might have to do things their way, but it was obvious to any fool it would be the wrong way.

"I think it's going to be the only revenge I'll get," Harlan explained quietly, coming up behind her as she knelt by the water. There was a pause and then he asked almost gently, "Was it really that bad?" There was a note of genuine concern in his voice now. Phoebe found it infinitely satisfying.

"Yes!" With a whirling movement she scooped a stream of icy water in his direction.

"Hey!" Harlan yelled as the water soaked his face and a fair amount of shirt front. He made a grab but Phoebe was already flying up the incline, releasing her tension in the laughter she left trailing behind. Jinx, not knowing the name of the new game, but willing to participate, raced madly along beside her, yelping joyously.

When Harlan appeared in the doorway several minutes later, Phoebe was busily engaged in mixing biscuit dough. She glanced across the room as his shadow fell over the wooden floor and was unable to contain a grin at the sight he made standing there in his soaked shirt, tackle box in one hand, and basket of fish in the other.

"You look as if you fell in," she told him sweetly, fingers busy in the dough. One glimpse of the laughing blue eyes had been enough to assure her the crisis was over. He had accepted her revenge in good humor and she was relieved. Harlan's eyes always told you exactly where you stood, she thought.

"Some man is going to have his hands very full keeping you under control," he remarked ruefully, striding through the room to pull a dry shirt out of his traveling bag. "I shall pity the poor guy. Even if he is a lot bigger than you!"

Phoebe chuckled. "I'm beginning to think I'll be better off with someone considerably smaller than me," she told him lightly.

"No, no, Phoebe," he corrected, flashing her his best shark smile as he buttoned the dry shirt. "You don't need someone who is too big or too small. You need someone who is exactly right for you."

Phoebe decided not to continue in the rather provocative direction the conversation was taking. She'd had enough for the moment. She needed time to recover from the surprising loss in the recent contest of wills between them. She had lost such battles with men before in the business world. Everyone lost there at one time or another. But she had never encountered a man who cared to enforce his mastery over her outside the corporate setting. The whole event had uncomfortable similarities to a conflict out of a romantic novel and Phoebe was rapidly coming to the conclusion that being mastered by a man was not all it was cracked up to be in the books she read—especially when the man didn't fit the proper physical image in the least and, furthermore, was extremely unlikely to fall head over heels in love with her!

chapter three

Harland built a pleasant, crackling fire after dinner and
Jinx wandered over to stretch out in front of the fireplace on the thin rug. His master groped around in a bag
and then produced an unexpected bottle of wine and a
jar of popcorn with the air of a magician. Phoebe
laughed with pleasure and the evening settled down
enjoyably. She crouched in front of the fire, wielding
the old-fashioned corn popper and dispensing the
results to dog and man alike. Jinx, it seemed, had a
passion for the stuff. When everyone except the dog had
eaten a sufficient quantity, she reclined against the base
of the chair Harlan was occupying and the three of them
gazed quietly into the fire, each thinking their own
thoughts. Phoebe had just finished a leisurely sip of
wine when she suddenly became aware of the fact that
Harlan's strong hand was toying very gently with her
tangled hair. She froze.

"Phoebe?" he questioned softly, hand moving
slightly.

"Yes?" She didn't move or turn to look at him.
Instead she launched into a private lecture to herself on
the fact that it wasn't in the least flattering to have a
man make overtures when one happened to be the only
woman for miles around!

"Are you going to holler rape to my aunt on Monday
morning just because I'm going to kiss you tonight?"
Harlan asked in a low, husky voice. The fingers of his

hand moved down to stroke the nape of her neck under the curving fall of dark hair.

Phoebe felt herself tremble. How was she going to handle this little twist, she wondered? After all, it certainly wasn't as if he were bowled over by her ravishing beauty or exquisite figure! Treat it lightly, she told herself. He surely wasn't laboring under a raging desire, she decided with a rueful smile so he wasn't likely to get out of hand. In a brisk, bracing tone she chided,

"Of course, I'm not going to scream 'rape' because we both know full well you aren't going to rape me! And if you're honest with yourself and me you'll admit you really don't even want to kiss me! Just because you're miles from your usual supply of small blonds, don't sacrifice your principles, Harlan!" She turned her head a fraction to glance up at him, willing him to smile in response.

"Do you always go around telling men what they want and don't want?" he inquired interestedly, his hand still at her nape. She watched his eyes and something she saw there made her worry for the first time. They weren't smiling back at her. In fact, the intensity which had crept into the blue gaze was altogether new. It reminded her of the rough way he had lectured her earlier about trying to make Richard jealous. Had she misjudged him badly? Put herself back into danger in a desperate attempt to flee it? But she still saw no viciousness or brutality in him. If she was very careful . . .

"Only occasionally," she said as lightly as possible, attempting a small, friendly smile. He didn't smile back, but the blue eyes warmed a degree or two.

"Only occasionally," he repeated thoughtfully, moving his hand to catch her chin between thumb and forefinger and thereby trap her wary gaze.

"I think you're lying to me again," he noted, one

russet brow quirking upward. "But this time I can see the truth in your eyes. I think you've had a lot of practice telling men what to do, haven't you?" He didn't sound angry or upset by the knowledge, Phoebe thought. He seemed more amused now, than anything else. Before she could respond he leaned down until his mouth was only inches above her own. "But you won't be giving me orders, even if you think they are for my own good! Not tonight. Not ever." He didn't raise his voice in the least but Phoebe heard the same implacability she had heard that afternoon when he had forced her to clean the fish.

Perhaps the easiest, least provocative move would be to simply give him a willing, lighthearted kiss, she thought as his head lowered further. He might be one of those men who felt challenged when a woman resisted. She hadn't personally encountered any, but they were supposed to be around somewhere! Most of the men she'd known simply drew back a little sulkily if a woman put her foot down and refused to get involved in an embrace—the drunk and vicious rapists of last night excluded! But Harlan bore no relation to them!

Wide-eyed, Phoebe felt her chin angled higher and his lips on hers. The caress began almost gently, searchingly, as if Harlan was merely curious and had decided to satisfy his mild interest in her.

For a frozen time Phoebe remained passive beneath the touch of his mouth, experiencing a strange curiosity herself. This man was so different from Richard! Then, very slowly she sensed a controlled demand begin to emanate from him, a demand that she respond. Before she could make up her flustered mind on how to deal with his increasing ardor, he suddenly broke off the kiss and lifted his head to study her flushed features in the firelight.

Without a word he removed her glasses and set them down on a small table beside the chair. Now what? Phoebe wondered, worried about the significance of the act more than she cared to admit. She had better move now to regain a measure of control over the situation! But as if sensing her determination, Harlan reached down, pulling her around to face him.

"Harlan!" she squeaked, startled to find herself kneeling between his blue-jeaned thighs. "Wait a minute, I . . ." But she wasn't allowed to finish her sentence. His mouth came down once again, this time on lips which had been open to protest and his tongue plunged urgently between them. Phoebe began to struggle in earnest. A kiss or two she would have been willing to forfeit, she told herself furiously, but Harlan had stepped too far out of bounds by this last action. Angrily she tried to free herself from the grip of his hands on her shoulders, twisting her head in an effort to evade his mouth. But he held her as if she were without any power at all.

"Relax," he soothed, his lips moving deliberately to her throat.

"Relax!" she yelped, outraged by the effort to cajole. "Things have gone far enough. Take your hands off me this minute!"

"We've barely begun," he pointed out with male logic, easing her backward onto the rug, disturbing Jinx who obligingly got to his feet and moved off to settle elsewhere. "Now hush and let yourself go. You'll enjoy it."

"Of all the arrogant, overbearing . . ." Phoebe got no further. An instant later she was flat on the rug, his lean weight cushioned by her full, gentle curves. My God! She thought irrationally, he weighs a ton! And she was grimly aware that he was making no effort to take

49

any of his own weight on his elbows. Instead he was using it to anchor her firmly beneath him.

"Harlan! That's enough! I mean it . . ." Again her words were cut off, this time by his mouth as he covered hers. Now she was vividly aware that he had banked some of the earlier demand she had sensed in him. Instead there was an insistent, sensuous, prodding quality. It was as if he were determined to stoke the embers of her passion until it flamed into life and matched his own.

With a deliberate, blatantly male move of sexual aggression he forced his leg between hers. The feeling of utter female helplessness which surged through Phoebe at the action swamped her and with a moan she began to respond to his warm, invading mouth. She felt the sheer masculine satisfaction in him at the small surrender and knew she had made a mistake. But it was too late to stop. She wanted to sample more of the passion which was beginning to flow through her veins like hot honey. Richard had never kissed her like this, she thought blindly. No one had ever kissed her quite like this! It made her feel womanly, warm, and wanted.

Dimly she felt Harlan's hands at the buttons of her shirt, but she couldn't bring herself to protest. She felt him undo first one, then another, and another until her rounded breasts were protected from him only by the thin lacy stuff of her bra which had its clasp in front. Would he discover that, she wondered dizzily? A second later she felt his fingers on it and then her breasts were free of any restriction as he deftly found the secret of the catch.

Harlan drew in his breath at the full softness of her, moving one hand to cup it gently, palming a nipple in a stroking, gentle fashion that made it harden.

"Ah, Phoebe, you're exactly what a man needs in

these cold mountains!" he breathed, lowering his lips to the tip of a breast and taking it into his mouth. "So soft and inviting . . ."

A log broke in the fireplace, sending a shower of sparks up the chimney and momentarily throwing an added light into the room. Phoebe opened dazed sea-green eyes to meet the passion in Harlan's blue gaze and somewhere in her reeling mind a tiny voice finally managed to make itself heard. She must put a stop to this! Harlan cared nothing for her! He was only amusing himself on a cold night with the only woman around!

"Please," Phoebe begged, knowing now she had no power to force him to cease his lovemaking. "Please, Harlan. Don't go any farther. Let me go."

"Why?" he questioned almost absently, his attention on the small hollow of her throat. She sensed his thumb continuing to move on a nipple and almost groaned with the sheer excitement of it. But he didn't really care for her! She must remember that!

"Because—because you don't love me!" she blurted in a kind of despair.

That halted him. His heavy, sinewy frame went still and he raised his head to look down at her, the ice of his eyes reflecting an unfathomable expression.

"Do you demand that all your lovers be head over heels in love with you before you'll go to bed with them?" he finally asked roughly.

"Oh, Harlan! Is it so wrong for a woman to want a man to love her before she takes such a risk?" Phoebe pleaded gently.

"You're worried about getting pregnant?" he queried gently.

"Among other things," she smiled tremulously.

"What other things?" He sounded curious, she

51

thought. But she also knew instinctively that the crisis was over. She could tell by the way the passion was fading from the blue eyes, replaced by a hint of humor and the curiosity she had noted. Unconsciously she breathed a small sigh of relief. He felt it and a tiny smile quirked the hard line of his mouth.

"I asked what else you were afraid of, Phoebe?" he reminded her.

Feeling more relaxed now, she smiled up at him with a touch of sauciness.

"Oh, the usual things a woman is afraid of with a passionate man," she quipped, feeling once again in charge. Harlan wasn't going to force himself on her. As long as she stayed firm in her resolve, he wouldn't carry his lovemaking any farther.

"You're afraid of being hurt emotionally?" he suggested.

"Of course! Remember I told you earlier today that I couldn't bear to have my heart broken when we return to Portland and you go back to your blond beauties?" Phoebe's blue-green eyes sparkled now with laughter.

"Are you admitting that I already have that much power over you?" he countered.

The humor vanished instantly from Phoebe's face. Just when you thought you had the man back in hand, he said something outrageous!

"You're twisting my words, Harlan," she said very firmly, surreptitiously attempting to close the front of her blouse. Without even remarking on the movement Harlan forbade it by the simple expedient of trapping both her hands under as he leaned on his forearms above her.

"We both know you're not going to rape me, Harlan Garand, so why continue to tease me like this?" she said, trying to make herself sound rational and not the least flustered.

"We both know that? Tell me, Phoebe Hampton, how do *you* know I won't take you here and now?" he challenged, a distinct glint lighting the blue eyes.

For a long instant Phoebe stared at him, unblinking, and then she smiled again, ever so slightly.

"You'll stop," she announced with a serene certainty. "I'm very sure that you are not a really brutal man. I've told you this is as far as I want to take matters and you'll go along with it, even if you're upset with me. I trust you."

He held himself very still above her for a long moment, watching her face intently as if searching for something there which persisted in eluding him. Phoebe tried to read the flickers of emotion moving in the ice-blue depths and failed.

"You trust me, do you?" he repeated slowly, consideringly.

Phoebe nodded mutely, afraid to answer lest her words disturb the delicate balance of the situation. She must do nothing now to taunt or tease. Not if she wanted to avoid spending the rest of the night in his arms! And she did want to avoid that, didn't she? Phoebe refused to go into the question any more deeply just then. Right now the important thing was to regain the safe level of companionship she and Harlan had enjoyed earlier in the day. His lovemaking was far too dangerous for her peace of mind!

"It seems to me that we should be able to exchange trust for trust, don't you agree?" Harlan asked, almost conversationally, but the blue eyes never released her.

"What—what are you talking about?" Phoebe whispered nervously.

"If you can trust me, I should be able to trust you. Tell me the truth about how you got to the cabin today,

Phoebe," he instructed suddenly forcefully.

"But, Harlan, I've told you the truth . . ." Phoebe began, feeling desperate.

"I don't understand it!" he muttered, abruptly rolling away from her and getting to his feet in a fluid motion. "How can you lie and look at me like that at the same time? I would have sworn . . ." He cut himself off and shook off the anger Phoebe had seen rising in his eyes.

She could only marvel at Harlan's abrupt mood shift as he strode toward the cot on the far side of the room. She fumbled with the buttons of her blouse as he undid the strings on the sleeping bag.

"With a little squeezing we can make this cot do for both of us," Harlan remarked, no sign of emotion in his tones now. "I intend to sleep on it, by the way. My recently demonstrated chivalry does not extend to surrendering the only bed in sight to you when there's no reason in the world we can't share it!" He tossed her his shark grin as he unrolled the bag.

Phoebe watched him cautiously. "That's all right. If you have any extra blankets, I'll take the rug here in front of the fireplace," she said in a studied, casual tone.

"Come now," he said bracingly, "I thought you trusted me!"

"Well, I do." Phoebe hesitated and then added in a very low voice, "Within reason."

He ignored the qualification. "It gets cold in these mountains at night and the floor isn't going to be particularly warm or comfortable," Harlan pointed out matter of factly.

"It's better than what I had last night," Phoebe remarked pertly, feeling pressured. She got stiffly to her feet, feeling almost dizzy from the activity.

"Yes. Last night." The words were bitten out in a

short manner which clearly demonstrated his opinion of her tale. "Why can't you tell me the truth about that, Phoebe?" He left the sleeping bag and moved to stand in front of her, one hand reaching out to lightly stroke the line of her jaw. "I'm no longer in the mood to strangle you as I was this morning. It will be safe to confess now," he coaxed.

"I thought you already knew the truth!" she quipped, making a production of finding her glasses and slipping them protectively into place.

"But I want to hear it from you," he insisted.

Phoebe sighed regretfully. "Let's dig out those extra blankets," she suggested grimly, turning away. Without a word he crossed the room to a storage closet and hauled out a variety of what looked like old wool military blankets. He helped her spread them out in front of the fireplace and then handed her a flashlight so she could make the necessary trip outside. Jinx went along to stand guard and Phoebe was grateful for the dog's presence. Being outdoors in the mountain darkness brought back unpleasant fears she had been able to ignore during the day.

The three occupants of the cabin settled down to sleep a short time later. Phoebe discovered within ten minutes that the floor was, indeed, going to prove uncomfortable as well as cold when the last of the fire died away, her practical voice added silently. She considered telling Harlan she was having second thoughts and was almost on the verge of saying something when his voice came from the far wall. It was laced with rueful amusement.

"Phoebe?"

"Yes?"

"There is just one thing I have to know."

"What's that, Harlan?"

"Do you have a lot of success at keeping your men in their proper place with that line?" She could sense his

55

smile in the darkness.

"What line?" she inquired innocently.

"That one about trusting the poor guy. It doesn't leave him a lot of options, you know!"

Phoebe gave a muffled giggle. "I have always found it quite effective," she told him demurely, wishing privately there really had been a variety of men needing to be kept in place. Or perhaps just one particular man . . .

"So we all obediently back off, control our raging ardor, and try to live up to your ridiculous trust in our honor!" There was laughter in Harlan's words. "The Third's been buying this line for some time now, I take it, since you say you haven't slept with him?"

"I don't think Richard sees it as a 'line' exactly," Phoebe explained carefully thinking of the few times he had actually attempted much of a pass. "He always seemed . . ." she broke off and tried again. "He didn't seem to mind . . ." Face it, she told herself sternly, Richard's lack of desire was one of the main reasons she had been unable to fall in love with the man!

"The Third is a fool. Come here, Phoebe." The laughter was gone from Harlan's voice now and in its place was a new, rough note of command.

"Why?" she demanded, startled.

"Because I've told you to. Come here, woman. Don't put me to the trouble of fetching you."

Phoebe lay frozen for a moment considering the change in the situation. Harlan sounded quite determined and she couldn't be at all certain whether or not he was teasing her. On the surface it didn't sound like it. The rather belated notion that she had pushed her luck too far occurred to Phoebe.

"Harlan . . ." She began carefully, not moving.

"Come here, Phoebe," he ordered softly. "I'm not going to tell you again."

She didn't doubt him. When he wished, thought Phoebe wryly as she unrolled herself from the blankets, Harlan Garand could assume command with an alarming authority. Unable to think of a clever way out of the tangle, she got to her feet. Deep down she kept telling herself that he wouldn't really force himself on her. But even as she reassured herself, a small voice asked if that was her real fear. Or was she afraid of wanting him to do exactly that?

She was still wearing the jeans and blouse in an attempt to keep warm. Now she wrapped one of the blankets around her and, clutching it tightly, trailed slowly over to stand beside the cot. In the dim light of the dying fire, Harland regarded her speculatively, blue eyes shadowed and mysterious. With an abrupt motion he flipped back the top of the down-filled bag. Phoebe saw he was sleeping in only his jockey shorts and she gulped, clinging more tightly to the blanket.

"Get in," he said almost tonelessly.

"Harlan, I . . ."

"I said, get in. But first take off your jeans. They'll be too uncomfortable to wear inside the bag."

A wave of panic washed over Phoebe as she stood there, shivering in her cold, bare feet. Harlan looked quite determined to enforce his order and she could see no effective way of fighting him. She was at his mercy, the mercy of the cold night, and the mercy of her own inner longing.

"Move, Phoebe. It's getting cold."

Phoebe's fingers went reluctantly to the button of her jeans and she stepped out of them under the shelter of the blanket. For once in her life she felt absolutely helpless to resist the will of a man and it was both frightening and exhilarating. Harlan watched her, never taking his eyes from her face. A moment later she slid down beside him, reveling in the warmth and fearing the worst. When his arm closed around her, his hand rested almost casually on the breasts she had freed earlier from the bra. Phoebe closed her eyes and waited for she knew not what.

"This is much better than the floor, isn't it?" he asked silkily.

"It's warmer," she agreed in a tiny voice as she lay curled into the heat of his body.

"And more comfortable?" he suggested coolly, daring her to disagree.

"Yes," she responded stiffly.

"You're wondering what happens next, aren't you?" he persisted wickedly.

"Yes." The words were barely a whisper.

"You," he informed her with a soft, mocking smile, "are just going to have to trust me!"

Sunlight, warm and cheery, wakened Phoebe on Sunday morning. She lay quietly for a moment, savoring the warmth of Harlan's unconscious embrace and then, very stealthily, unzipped the sleeping bag. The easiest thing to do, she decided, was to be up and dressed before her host awoke. She spent almost five whole minutes slipping the zipper down notch by notch and then began to slide with utmost caution until her toes were out from under the weight of Harlan's leg. Delicately she edged his arm upward, about to slip from beneath it when with a sleepy laugh Harlan came awake in a hurry, clasping her rounded body firmly and tucking her back into the warm bag. When she was safely settled against him again, he lifted himself on one elbow and leaned his head down to kiss her slowly and lazily, showing no consideration at all for the effects of his rasping morning beard against her soft skin. The blue eyes glittered with humor as he regarded his wide-eyed victim.

"You have an interesting knack of looking slightly

astonished whenever things don't go the way you planned them," he chuckled. "It's a temptation to disrupt your schemes just to see that look. Do you normally get your own way in most things?"

"*Normally*," Phoebe stressed, struggling to a sitting position and fixing him with her severest frown, "There aren't that many people trying to get in my way!"

"Don't frown at me like that," he protested. "Didn't I behave myself last night and let you sleep in peace?"

"After terrifying me first!" she retorted waspishly, her eyes going to the tousled red hair.

"Didn't the Third ever terrify you just the least little bit?"

Phoebe's frown became even more severe as she scrambled around for her glasses. She had no idea why he kept mentioning Richard!

"Richard Elton Chambers III is, above all else, a gentleman!" Phoebe informed Harlan in a haughty tone, looking down her nondescript nose. "He wouldn't think of doing anything like that!"

"He doesn't know what he's been missing," Harlan remarked feelingly. "You were perfectly fashioned for cuddling on a cold night, Phoebe Hampton," he grinned. "All nice and round and warm and soft . . ." He broke off, apparently amused by the rising tide of color in her face. "As you said, the man must be very dull, indeed!"

Phoebe shrugged. "I expect it comes from having the proper amount of money and the right background," she admitted, taking advantage of his relaxed grip to swing her legs over the edge of the cot and pull on her jeans quickly. She felt much more in control when she was fully dressed.

"You think dullness is an inherited characteristic of someone who is financially successful?" Harlan asked interestedly from his position in the sleeping bag.

"Not necessarily. My brother is a self-made man and he's not dull in the least, although I may be somewhat prejudiced!" Phoebe smiled thoughtfully, walking across the room to refold the blanket she had left in front of the fireplace. "But maybe that's the difference."

"What is?"

"Whether or not a person has made their money or been born into it."

"The Third was born into his, I take it?"

Phoebe nodded. "Oh yes. He's the third, remember." Phoebe stepped over to the door to open it for a pleading Jinx. "Next time I get involved I think I shall make an effort to be sure he comes from a background more similar to my own. I would never have fit into Richard's world anyway. Still, I must admit, it was nice while it lasted!" She thought briefly of how gorgeous Richard was in full evening dress. It was a definite shame the man's personality did not match his looks!

"Sounds to me as if you may have been guilty of using the poor man," Harlan announced. "He must have been getting some feedback from you if he was inspired to offer marriage!" Phoebe heard the disapproval in his voice and shook her head firmly.

"Never. I gave him no reason to think I was ever that attracted to him. To tell you the truth, I was as surprised as anyone when he asked me to marry him! Surely he must have known that something was missing from our relationship, pleasant though it was."

"Maybe he felt the spark of passion and restrained himself in the hopes you would someday return the feeling," Harlan suggested, climbing out of the sleeping bag unself-consciously and stepping into his jeans. Phoebe glanced away hurriedly. When she looked in his direction again he was busy rolling the bag.

"No, I don't think one could say that the Third was

motivated by any strong romantic impulses," she mused with a small smile. "What that man needs is an attractive ornament for a wife. Why he thought I'd suit the role is beyond me, although I must admit I was flattered!"

"You don't think you're the ornament type?" Harlan inquired, sounding intrigued as he pulled a clean shirt out of his traveling bag.

"Could I borrow an extra shirt if you have it?" Phoebe asked. "This one is beginning to itch!"

Without a word, Harlan tossed her an old work shirt which Phoebe deftly caught. "Thanks, I'll wash mine today and then I'll be able to give this one back to you!"

"You didn't answer my question," he pointed out.

"About being an oranment?" she sighed. "I would have thought it was obvious! Of course I'm not the type! I told you yesterday, I plan to use my cooking to catch my man!" She flashed him a grin and opened the door to follow Jinx outside, feeling that she had managed to put the peculiar relationship between Harlan and herself back on a safe, bantering basis.

Forty-five minutes later, neatly shaved and looking the picture of masculine vitality, Harlan polished off the last of his crisp bacon and complimented Phoebe on breakfast.

"I suppose," he added, chuckling, "I should be grateful I haven't had to beat you to make you assume the traditional feminine role around the cabin!"

"I do have a sense of fair play, you know. I'm quite aware of the fact that I barged in on your weekend, that I'm eating your food, and have otherwise been a general nuisance," Phoebe smiled back. "I'm willing to try and repay some of the hospitality, no matter how reluctantly it may have been extended! What's on the agenda for this morning? Are you going to fish again?"

"I was going to suggest a hike down to the falls and

back. It will work up an appetite for lunch. Besides, Jinx needs the exercise. He's going to get fat if you keep sneaking him scraps under the table like that!''

Phoebe withdrew her hand guiltily and then laughed. "A hike would be great," she agreed, getting to her feet to clear the table. "We'd better take advantage of the sunshine while we have it. This being Oregon, the rain could arrive at any moment," she added sweetly.

"That's simply a myth Oregonians tell Californians. It discourages them from emigrating," he informed her loftily.

The walk to the point in the stream where the rushing water cascaded whitely over a mighty outcropping took most of the morning, but it was worth it. Phoebe was thoroughly enjoying having the day in the woods and Harlan Garand all to herself. Common sense, of course, intervened from time to time reminding her that it wasn't going to last long, but Phoebe decided she would take advantage of the pleasant excitement which seemed to be associated with Harlan's presence. She would be careful, especially tonight, but the temptation to play with the fire of his personality was hard to resist. The sunlight slanted down through the trees, removing the morning chill, and lending a special clarity to the fresh mountain air. Reality would return soon enough.

Phoebe was in the midst of preparing a late luncheon after the return from the morning walk when Jinx began barking furiously. Harlan was outside collecting firewood for the coming evening. Jinx, who had been sitting in the open doorway sunning himself suddenly leaped to his feet and crossed the porch at a dead run. Phoebe glanced at him as he disappeared and then went back to her salad making. The dog had probably sensed a deer and the hunter instinct in him had leaped to the fore.

Several minutes later the barking ceased abruptly and

Phoebe grinned to herself. Poor Jinx. He'd probably lost the deer and would be back shortly, pretending nothing at all had happened.

But it wasn't Jinx who next appeared in the cabin doorway. It was Harlan, looking quite scruffy. His short red hair was awry and there was a good deal of dust on his jeans. He stood silently regarding Phoebe with a strange expression in his blue eyes, as if he hadn't seen her properly until now.

"What's wrong?" she asked, the faint trace of astonishment he had commented on earlier much in evidence as she peered at him questioningly through the lenses of her glasses.

"Is Jinx okay?" she prodded, facing him with one hand holding the knife she had been using to spread mustard.

"Jinx," said Harlan very distinctly, "is fine." He glanced back over his shoulder and then returned his level stare to meet her curious one. "Could you please," he said carefully, "run through your story of the Great Escape briefly?"

"Why?" Phoebe asked, floored by the unexpected request.

"Just the part about how you got away," he specified, ice eyes pinning her, demanding an answer.

"Well, one of them had gone outside to get more wood for the fire. They had freed me to prepare some dinner and I had a pot of water boiling on the stove. It was to be used to cook the noodles for one of those package dinners they had brought along. I had a sudden thought that I might not get a better chance and I just—just tossed the whole pot of water at the man who was supposed to be keeping an eye on me. He screamed. It was awful! I ran out the back door and into the woods. I kept going, listening for the sound of water. They tried to follow but I wasn't afraid of getting lost and they were, I guess. At any rate they gave up after a while. I knew I couldn't use the road but I had read somewhere that one could follow a stream off a mountain. Harlan, why are you asking me such a question now?"

"Because there is a gentleman outside who bears a strong resemblance to a boiled lobster asking for you . . ." He broke off abruptly as Phoebe went very white very quickly. The knife in her hand dropped unheeded to the floor.

"Hey! Honey, it's okay! It's all under control, I promise you!" Harlan leaped forward, the strange expression he had worn earlier giving way to a heart-warming concern. Phoebe manged a shaky smile.

"Sorry. It's only that I had almost put the whole mess out of my mind, telling myself I'd worry about it on Monday. I felt so safe here with you and Jinx . . ." Phoebe wished she could keep her lower lip from trembling.

"You *are* safe," Harlan swore with great feeling, holding her firmly by the shoulders. "Perfectly safe. I've got the guy tied up nice and tight. Jinx is standing guard. The way the man was sneaking up on the cabin he's lucky he hasn't suffered a good deal more than he already has! Neither Jinx nor I take kindly to shifty types!" Harlan's tones were ruefully soothing as he held her close against his dusty shirt, one large hand gently stroking her thick, rich hair. "When the fight was over and I asked him what the hell he thought he was doing he said something abut looking for a 'friend,' a female friend, at that! I didn't mean to startle you so. I was trying to be cool about the whole thing, you see, because I'm in a position of having made a ghastly mistake and now I've got to figure out a way to apologize!"

Phoebe found herself chuckling into his shirt. "You don't owe me anything in the way of apologies," she murmured. "In the beginning, I thought it might be pleasant to have you find out the truth but you've more than made up for whatever you thought of me by providing me with one of the most interesting weekends I've had in a long time!'' Privately, Phoebe decided it was the best weekend of her entire life but the practical side of her nature warned her to keep things light. She *had* to keep things light!

"How can you say that?" Harlan groaned. "I made all those terrible accusations! No wonder you thought my ego was so damn inflated." He looked momentarily disgusted with himself and Phoebe found herself laughing.

"You gave me shelter and food when I needed them badly. I had the protection of you and your noble hound. I've learned how to clean fish and you topped everything off very pleasantly by making a pass which did wonders for my feminine ego. Then you capped even that by proving yourself a true gentleman and not taking advantage of me! Throw in the excitement of the initial kidnapping and the fact that you've caught one of the villains and what more could a woman ask for out of a weekend fling?" Phoebe stepped back in the circle of his arms and blinked at him through glasses which had been tilted slightly askew.

Harlan shook his head uncomprehendingly. "Incredible," he mumbled to himself and then his old familiar grin flashed into place as he caught her chin between thumb and forefinger. "Treasure that one moment of my gentlemanly behavior last night, Phoebe," he advised. "I've made a couple of mistakes with you which I don't intend to repeat in the future! One of them was thinking you could lie to me. I should have known that with those eyes you could never hide the truth for long. No wonder I felt so confused every time I looked at you and asked for the real story!"

He paused, still looking down at her. "The second mistake was in letting you talk me out of making love to you last night. I won't repeat that one, either!"

chapter four

Phoebe's response to Harlan's words would not, she felt, have done her credit in front of her staff who held the view that she could handle almost any situation. He must be teasing, of course, but his words left her momentarily breathless and mute. Before she could gather the courage to ask him what he meant he was tugging her along behind him as he led the way outdoors.

"Come on and see if this joker looks familiar. We really are going to be in a fix if Jinx and I have cornered an innocent victim! Of course, now we've got a trespassing charge," Harlan remarked, holding her wrist in a firm grip.

Phoebe stared down at the infuriated man lying trussed on the ground. How could she have been so foolish as to get into a truck with such a creature? If she hadn't been so angry at the failure of the rental car and anxious to get to her destination she would have exercised more common sense! She had done a fair amount of damage with the hot water but remembering the fact that she had been in fear of being raped or even killed, she couldn't feel too sorry about it. Harlan idly fingered the small gun which Phoebe recognized with a shiver.

"Jinx found him hiding in the woods at the edge of the clearing. The guy was so frightened of the dog he forgot to use this." Harlan wrapped the weapon in a handkerchief and smiled unpleasantly. Phoebe prudently decided not to inquire into the cause of his humor.

"This is the man, all right—one of them. The other was bigger." Phoebe said quietly, looking away from the fury and hate in the kidnapper's face.

"So much for the remainder of my bachelor weekend in the mountains," Harlan noted absently, studying his captive. "We'd better get going. I've already done enough to impede justice by making it impossible for you to report the kidnapping, Phoebe. I don't want to add any other sins to my growing roster." He leaned down to pat an alert Jinx who was now all business as he stood guard over his victim. "Keep an eye on him, my friend, while Phoebe and I get packed." Harlan glanced at Phoebe. "Come on, honey, let's move." He suited action to words and headed toward the cabin.

Phoebe turned dutifully to follow and then stopped for one last speculative look at her former tormentor. It was a mistake. The small cruel eyes were fixed on her as if she were potential prey. For the first time, the man spoke, his voice sounding harsh and raspy, a sound she remembered so well from Friday night.

"Max is still free and clear," he snarled in a hoarse whisper. "He'll get you, you bitch! I swear it!"

"Care to repeat that to a police officer?" Phoebe asked spiritedly before turning firmly on her heel and moving quickly toward the porch. The thought of the other kidnapper running around loose wasn't a pleasant one but she told herself that if the one named Max had any common sense—and he had seemed the more intelligent of the two—he would be in the next state by now.

The ride back to Portland was accomplished in what Phoebe privately thought must have been record time. The captive was left to fend for himself in the rear of the vehicle with Jinx who growled every time the man

67

moved. The fear of dogs seemed genuine and the sight of the big black Lab sitting so alertly beside him was all the intimidation needed to keep him quiet.

The encounter with the police went efficiently, much to Phoebe's amazement. She had half expected that no one would believe the outlandish story, but Harlan's presence seemed to lend her some credibility although he was right when he had remarked that the forces of the law were not going to look kindly upon his unwitting impeding of their work. One older, grizzled detective saw fit to give the younger man the sharp edge of his tongue in a scathing tone which Phoebe had a hunch was used indiscriminately on any who fell within his jurisdiction from mayors to bums. Harlan took the criticism with a properly sober expression and then spoiled the effect by saying,

"I'm sorry, sir, but the minute Phoebe walked into camp I ceased functioning in my normal rational manner." He glanced at a reddening Phoebe and grinned unrepentantly. The flush deepened as the detective turned to look her over appraisingly.

"And as for you, young woman, I should think you would have had more sense than to accept a ride on the highway like that! Don't you ever read the newspapers?"

"Yes, sir," Phoebe whispered, guiltily, avoiding Harlan's eyes.

"Then you know that the proper procedure is to stay with the car, doors and windows locked, and wait for a passing highway patrol car!"

"Yes, sir," she whispered again. She didn't need to be lectured on the subject, Phoebe thought bitterly. It had been a stupid stunt and it had only been sheer luck she had come out of the situation unscathed. Of course, if she hadn't been so foolish she would never have met

Harlan Garand and that experience had been worth a good deal . . .

With a certain fascination, Phoebe went through the routine of police work. She gave her statement in as much detail as possible, doing her best to describe the other hunter in the truck. The police seemed to agree with her private analysis that he would probably flee the state. Harlan listened attentively when this particular probability was discussed but volunteered no comment. Phoebe had the impression he wasn't altogether convinced.

Patiently they took her through every detail, digging out maps, and drawing circles on them in an effort to estimate how far she might have walked before stumbling onto Harlan's cabin.

"We'll start searching for the place where you were held this afternoon, Miss Hampton," she was told. The detective yelled instructions over his shoulder to have the sheriff's department contacted.

During the entire procedure Harlan never left her side and Phoebe found herself surprisingly grateful for the support. When they were at last excused, he escorted her back out to where the jeep had been illegally parked with Jinx inside and announced he would drive her home.

"The first thing I'm going to do is take a shower, a *hot* shower, and wash my hair!" Phoebe informed him, climbing into the seat and greeting the dog affectionately. "Not that I wasn't impressed by the novelty of bathing in a cold stream, but there is definitely something to be said for the amenities of civilization!"

She gave directions to her apartment building in downtown Portland and settled back as Harlan switched on the engine. He seemed unnaturally quiet during the drive to the charming older building which overlooked one of the city's numerous parks. She found herself chatting freely in an effort to cover the silence. It was necessary to do so because she had no intention of allowing the man to think she was in the least depressed about the imminent conclusion of the spectacular weekend. All too soon he was halting the vehicle in front of the familiar red brick building with its sunny bay windows. Summoning a bright smile and an appropriately casual remark, she turned in her seat to say goodbye to Harland and Jinx.

"I want both of you to know that I've had a very exciting weekend and I shall be happy to recommend the accommodations to the travel agency that booked them for me," she began cheerily.

"Good," Harlan grinned, climbing out of his side of the jeep and motioning Jinx to stay behind. "I thought for a moment there the primitive aspects might have put you off the place!"

"All part of the atmosphere," Phoebe said airily, thinking it was very polite of him to see her to the door.

"I'll have to see the landlady about the key. It was in my purse, which, as far as I know, is back at that cabin," she told him as she jumped out of the jeep to join him on the sidewalk.

"That will teach you to accept rides from strangers . . ."

"Please! I don't need any more lectures read to me on that subject!" Phoebe informed him with a trace of tartness. What did he and the police think she was? Stupid?

"And if you hadn't decided to take off by yourself to spend a day at the coast you wouldn't have been driving alone in the evening in the first place!" Harlan plowed on, warming to the topic as he took Phoebe's arm and guided her forcibly toward the neat little entrance of the apartment building.

"I had every right in the world to take off by myself Friday night," she interrupted, ruffled.

"It never would have happened if you'd belonged to me instead of the Third!" Harlan shot back with the air of a debater who has scored a major point.

"I don't belong to the Third! And what's that got to do with anything? I would still have the right to spend a weekend by myself, regardless of whom I happened to be dating!" Phoebe badly wished the conversation hadn't begun to deteriorate. It would have been so much nicer to have concluded things on a light note!

"Not if you belonged to me," he informed her loftily, "my woman would not have found herself free on a Friday night, you see. She wouldn't find herself free until the next morning. Then, possibly, she might be allowed to go home and feed her bird!"

"Do you always force your dates to stay overnight?" Phoebe snapped, feeling much flustered by the wickedly male expression he was directing down at her.

"Only the cuddly ones."

"Harlan!"

Before Phoebe could continue to berate him for his teasing, he was drawing her to a halt in front of the door marked "Manager." But as he lifted his hand to knock it was flung open to reveal an elderly lady in a stained painting smock who peered at them with snapping grey eyes.

"Phoebe! I thought I heard voices out here! Where have you been all weekend? You were supposed to be back Saturday. You know I like my tenants to alert me when they're planning on being away for an extended period . . ." She broke off suddenly to frown up at Harlan.

"Who's this?" she demanded, wiping her hands

absently on the smock.

"Harlan, this is my landlady, Mrs. Morrison. She, uh, paints. Very well, too," Phoebe smiled at the thin woman, noting the streak of chromium yellow in the halo of curly white hair. "This is Harlan Garand, Mrs. Morrison, a friend of mine."

"Hmmm. Close friend?" Mrs. Morrison inquired, eyeing Harlan shrewdly.

"Very close," Harlan supplied agreeably, saving Phoebe from having to answer. There was an instant's silence while each appraised the other and then he asked politely, "Will I do?"

"You'll do." The woman turned her piercing gaze on Phoebe. "I like him a hell of a lot better than the other one!" she proclaimed as if it were the last word on the subject. Phoebe wished very badly the floor would open and allow her to descend into the basement.

"Mrs. Morrison!" she begged, well aware of the amusement in Harlan's smile. "How—how did you know I had been gone?" she asked lamely, trying desperately to switch the subject.

"That damn bird of yours, of course. Started yelling Saturday afternoon and has kept it up off and on all day today. Could hear him clear out in the hallway, according to the Thompsons," Mrs. Morrison told her grimly.

"I'm very sorry," Phoebe began hurriedly. "I know Ferd gets a bit temperamental when I'm not around for long periods of time. I'll go right up to him," she edged away, reaching out to pluck at Harlan's sleeve. He remained standing where he was, giving a fair imitation of a rock.

"You're forgetting that you've lost your key," he reminded her gently.

"Oh, yes," Phoebe turned back to her landlady. "I've lost my purse and I wondered if you could get me

72

another key? I could have it copied in the morning . . .''

"How did you lose your purse?" came the predictable question.

"I'll tell you later, Mrs. Morrison. I really think I ought to be getting along to Ferd. He'll be in a frenzy!"

"True." The woman disappeared inside the apartment and returned a few minutes later with a key. "Here you go. Now, I'll want to hear what happened, later, understand?" White brows lowered severely.

"Yes, Mrs. Morrison," Phoebe smiled in relief. "I'll tell you all about it, I promise!"

"All about it?" Harlan inquired interestedly as they headed for the elevator.

"Well, I expect I'll have to expurgate certain portions," Phoebe admitted with a wry chuckle. "But I'm sure Mrs. Morrison's imagination will fill in the blanks!" The elevator arrived and she hesitated before stepping inside. "There's no need to take me any farther," she said carefully, not wanting him to feel in the least *obligated*. "I appreciate everything you've done for me this weekend and I'll always be grateful to both you and Jinx for catching that awful man . . ." Phoebe hurried into the elevator which showed signs of wanting to close. It was an older model and she had learned it was best not to argue with it. "Thanks again, Harlan. I had a very exciting time . . ." Phoebe stopped in midsentence as Harlan stepped into the elevator.

"There's really no need . . ." she began nervously.

"Hush, Phoebe. I'm going to come up to your apartment. We have things to discuss and besides, I want to meet Ferd." The amusement in his eyes confused her. Harlan was playing havoc with her nerves, she decided, in a way Richard had never succeeded in doing. She must be very careful, she told herself firmly. There could be no future for her with a man who much pre-

73

ferred the fragile blonds of the world. She knew instinctively she should protect herself as much as possible by ending things quickly. The silence which pervaded the elevator for the remainder of the trip to the fourth floor didn't appear to phase Harlan at all. He seemed quite at ease and when the door slid open in its creaky fashion, he took her key, checked the number, and started across the hall to the proper entrance.

"I'm curious to see what your place looks like," he told her as he twisted the knob and opened the door. "I have an inner vision of how you would decorate a home and I want to see how far off it is!"

"Oh. Well, I suppose . . ." Phoebe stopped as the sound of the opening door set off an incredible screech from within the apartment.

"Ferd!" She rushed inside, heading toward the cage hanging in a corner of the living room, the occupant of which was madly racing back and forth across a wooden perch while yelling at the top of his tiny lungs.

"Ferd, behave yourself! I'm home now and you've still got plenty of water and seed so control your feelings or I won't let you outside the cage!"

Phoebe stood for a minute, eyeball to eyeball with the infuriated parakeet, and then stepped back as Ferd slunk away to the far side of his cage, mumbling evilly.

"I have to be firm with him. He knows I got him on sale an can't return him to the pet shop!" Phoebe explained as she straightened.

"He looks vicious," Harlan observed, walking across the hardwood floor with its brilliant throw rugs to examine the bird more closely.

"He is," Phoebe assured him, surveying the blue and white creature affectionately. One bright eye regarded her balefully and then it switched to the man beside her.

"Fee, fie, fo, fum" roared Ferd in his high-pitched voice, "I smell the blood of an Oregonian!"

74

"Now, Ferd, remember what I said," Phoebe admonished him severely. "Do you want out of that cage or not?"

Ferd instantly leaped to the bar nearest his door and looked out expectantly, his attention completely refocused on an object a good deal more important than Harlan—freedom.

"Do you think it's safe to let him out?" Harlan asked apprehensively as Phoebe unlocked the cage and inserted a finger toward Ferd.

"You're bigger than he is," she pointed out as Ferd climbed regally aboard and allowed himself to be removed from his residence.

"Just make sure you keep him out of my way or I'll fetch Jinx to protect me," Harlan ordered, glancing around the room appreciatively, taking in the romantic wicker furniture and the multitude of hanging plants. A small smile crossed his face as he strolled over to the elegant fan chair and gingerly lowered himself into it.

"Don't worry, it wouldn't dare collapse beneath you," Phoebe assured him, allowing Ferd to transfer to her shoulder where he used his beak to tug ruthlessly at strands of hair. "Would you like a cup of tea or something?" she added, feeling somewhat at a loss as to how to handle him now that the man showed every sign of making himself at home on her territory.

"That would be nice. I'll fix it while you have your shower," Harlan replied easily, eyeing her disheveled appearance politely. "Then we'll go have a bite to eat at that pizza place I saw down the street. It's almost dinner time!"

The situation was getting a little out of hand, Phoebe thought anxiously.

"Harlan," she said delicately, "This is the night Richard is supposed to come by for his answer . . ."

"I remember." He may have remembered. He

75

obviously didn't particularly care, she thought, beginning to grow irritated.

"Well, I don't think it would be very hospitable to have you here when he arrives," she clarified firmly. "Regardless of the answer I'm going to give him!"

"Don't worry about Richard, honey. I intend to make the matter very plain to him," Harlan said calmly.

"What matter?" Phoebe demanded forebodingly, frowning at him.

"What a pair!" Harland leaned back in the fantasy chair and eyed the two confronting him. "It's clear Jinx and I are going to have our work cut out for us!"

"Harlan, will you please explain what's going on? Why are you sticking around?" she asked bluntly.

"I'm sticking around to make sure you give the Third his answer," he smiled.

"I'm quite capable of giving it to him alone!"

"Apparently you aren't or you wouldn't be having to repeat it. If you'd been firm the first time, he wouldn't be coming by tonight to see if you've changed your mind, would he?" Harland asked reasonably, stretching his legs out in front of him as he eyed her growing annoyance. "What time was he due to receive his second set of walking papers, anyway?"

"Don't talk like that!" Phoebe bit out. "Richard is a very nice man who has done me a great honor by asking me to marry him. The least I can do is try and let him down as gently as possible. I certainly don't intend to be rude about the matter!" She glanced at the digital clock on the radio. "He'll be here at seven-thirty," she answered his question belatedly.

"That gives us an hour and a half to get a bite to eat. If you hurry the shower, we'll be back here in plenty of time."

Phoebe stared at him, brow furrowed in concentration for a long moment. It was plain the man wasn't going to leave until he desired to do so. It would probably be safer to get him back outside the apartment. She might have a chance at keeping him from getting back in. Finally Phoebe nodded.

"All right," she agreed rather shortly, and turned to head down the hall to the bathroom, determinedly ignoring the suspiciously bland smile on Harlan's face as he watched her leave. The man was impossible! One minute she felt in danger of falling for him and the next he made her want to strike him with the nearest large object! She wondered forlornly if the little blonds had any better luck keeping him in line and in the next breath wished there weren't any little blonds at all in the picture!

The pizza was very good and Phoebe had a glass of the red wine that Harlan ordered to go with it but nothing could make her forget the upcoming interview with Richard Chambers. As the time wore on, she felt herself growing increasingly nervous which, in turn, only served to heighten her irritability. Disgustedly she told herself she wasn't behaving in her normal manner at all. Remaining largely oblivious to Harlan's deliberately casual conversation, Phoebe set her mind to work on the problem of getting rid of her escort before Richard arrived. Harlan showed every sign of carrying out his threat and attaching himself to her for the remainder of the evening. She couldn't fathom why he should want to do so, but there was no doubt about the awkwardness which was going to develop if she didn't detach him soon.

It was seven-fifteen by the time Harlan walked her back to the apartment door, having insisted on stopping by the jeep to give Jinx a brief break. Phoebe had no luck in convincing him to leave her at the elevator and when she fished her new key out of the pocket he immediately removed it from her hand and proceeded to open her door. Firmly she stepped just over the threshold and turned to face him, a polite office smile on her expressive mouth.

"Thank you very much for a pleasant evening and a most interesting weekend . . ." she began formally.

"You must be mistaking me for the Third," he told her casually, taking a determined step forward. It had the effect of driving her back a pace. "Save your polite farewells for him. I don't intend to leave yet."

"Now, Harlan, it's getting late. Richard will be here any minute and the two of us have something very important to discuss, as you know full well. I should think a man of your intelligence would understand that this is not the sort of social conversation which will be improved by adding a third party!" she snapped waspishly, losing patience with the man filling her doorway.

"Don't worry, honey. I'll handle everything," Harlan said soothingly, forcing her back completely from the door and immediately following up his victory by moving into the room. "Have a seat while we wait for the Third. You know, I really like this place. It looks exactly as it should. Both sides of your nature are here. Lots of romance in the living room and possibly the bedroom . . ." he broke off to lift an inquiring eyebrow, inviting her to confirm his guess. When Phoebe simply glared, he continued, "And the practical streak is represented in your tidy little kitchen." He nodded as if congratulating himself on having analyzed her so well and then he grasped her wrist and pulled her along behind him toward the settee.

"Harlan, I've been very patient with you," Phoebe started wrathfully, trying with a total lack of success to free herself. "But now you're going too far! Please leave this instant! I won't have you here when Richard arrives and that's final!" She was tugged down alongside him on the pillows.

"Honey, you're going to have to learn that I don't always follow orders very well. I'm more accustomed to giving them, you see. So why don't you relax and we can wait for Richard in a more peaceful atmosphere."

"Stop talking to me as if I were a child! You have no right in this apartment and I refuse to tolerate your unwelcome presence one more minute . . ." Phoebe was halted in midstride as the doorbell rang demandingly. She sat staring at Harlan with a stunned expression.

"He's early," she whispered helplessly, feeling the outrage seep out of her and a strong sensation of inevitability take over.

"I'll let him in," Harlan offered, getting to his feet.

"Harlan, no!"

But it was too late. Harlan was already at the door, throwing it open with a grand gesture as he greeted the startled Richard with a jovial smile. Only the ice in his eyes gave any indication that the smile was not altogether genuine, Phoebe thought grimly.

Tall, dark haired, and very good looking, Richard Elton Chambers III stood staring at the lean, redheaded man facing him. In the strained atmosphere Phoebe couldn't help but be aware of the differences in the two men. Richard was his usual elegant self, attired now in casual slacks and corduroy sport coat which had the effect of making Harlan's faded jeans and workshirt even more rough looking than they normally would have appeared. With his height, Richard always looked good, Phoebe thought, wishing mightily she could have fallen in love with the man. But seeing him next to Harlan she knew even more clearly than before that something important was missing in Richard's makeup —something very apparent in Harlan's. There was no question which of the two men dominated the scene. And Phoebe found herself resenting Harlan's easy self-assertion.

"I'm Harlan Garand and you don't need to introduce yourself," he was saying helpfully to the taller man, waving him casually into the room as if it were his apartment and not Phoebe's. "You're Richard Elton Chambers the Third. I'm pleased to meet you," he added with due politeness, holding out his hand which was reluctantly shaken by a confused looking Richard.

"I see. The name is familiar," Richard said with great civility, Phoebe thought. "You're a friend of Phoebe's?"

Harlan took in the full effect of the other man, running an obviously perusing eye from the top of Richard's carefully styled hair to the tip of his expensive Italian leather loafers. Then he smiled and Phoebe, recognizing the smile instantly, unstuck herself from the settee and bounded forward in an attempt to forestall his next words. But she was too late. Much too late.

"You could say that," Harlan answered Richard's question. "We just spent the weekend together."

For an instant the only sound in the room was a furious little squeak from Phoebe. Then she found her tongue and rushed toward Richard, taking a grip on his arm and leading him into the living room.

"Don't listen to him! He's got a very strange sense of humor. What he means is, he gave me a lift out of the mountains after these two awful men gave me a lift on the highway and then kidnapped me! Oh, it's a long story . . ." she began desperately.

"Phoebe, what's going on here? Where have you been all weekend? I tried to call you this morning and there was no answer. Where did you run into this Mr., uh, Garand, anyway?"

Poor Richard, Phoebe groaned inwardly. He must be hopelessly confused.

"Sit down, Richard," she ordered gently. "I'll fix

you a drink and explain the whole thing . . ." He would understand once she had a chance to outline the sequence of events logically. Richard was a very logical man. It was how he ran his company—logically.

"You tell him all about it, Phoebe," Harlan instructed from behind her. "I'll get the drink. You'll probably need one, too, I imagine."

"But you don't know where everything is . . ." she protested, turning to fix him with a furious expression.

"Now, honey, there's no point in trying to make Richard think we're not well acquainted. I'm sure he's grasping the situation in detail!" With that, Harlan disappeared in the direction of the kitchen and began opening cupboard doors energetically.

"Oh, Richard, I'm so sorry everything's so confused, but there is a reasonable explanation, I promise!"

"That man . . ." Richard began tenaciously.

"Yes, I know. He can be very annoying. The fact of the matter is, I owe him a debt of gratitude, though. I might still be trying to find my way down that mountain if I hadn't run into his cabin, you know. And that terrible hunter might have found me and done something drastic!"

"Okay, Phoebe. I can see you've been through an upsetting experience. Take it from the top and explain to me exactly what did happen."

Phoebe smiled, thankful for Richard's calm, understanding approach. She drew a deep breath, determined to get through as much of the story as possible before Harlan returned. She could hear the clink of glasses from the kitchen.

Concentrating totally on the good looking, if rather perplexed, man in front of her, she told Richard the story quickly and succinctly, glossing over the weekend she had spent with Harlan with the comment that she had stumbled into his camp and he had given her a ride back to Portland the next day. But Richard Elton Chambers III had not gotten to be Managing Director of the Portland branch of the family's timber firm on his looks alone.

"You arrived Saturday morning at the cabin and that man didn't bring you back until this afternoon?" he asked slowly.

"Well, you see, he didn't believe my story right away. It wasn't until that terrible man came creeping around, the one I threw the boiling water on, that Harlan realized I was telling the truth." Phoebe watched Richard with a hopeful expression.

"Phoebe, this is all a little hard to absorb . . . '

"Exactly my opinion on Saturday morning, Chambers," Harlan agreed genially, carrying a tray of drinks into the living room with the air of a gracious host. "You can see why I hesitated to take Phoebe at face value when she appeared on my doorstep at six o'clock in the morning with such a ridiculous tale! Of course, after I had gotten to know her better, much better, I realized she was telling the truth." He set the tray down on the glass-topped rattan coffee table and handed a glass to Richard.

"I would have trusted her at once!" Richard declared firmly. Phoebe smiled at him gratefully.

"You would?" Harlan asked with obvious interest. He glanced speculatively at Phoebe who wanted to yell at him abusively. "Oh, I agree she looks fairly harmless right now. But you should have seen her this weekend with her hair all tangled and her jeans a mess. She had lost a button off her blouse which gave her a very disreputable looking décolletage. All in all, she appeared quite abandoned on Saturday morning. If you'd been in my place you'd have wanted to see how much more abandoned she'd get by Saturday night. It's no wonder I waited a while to bring her home!"

"Harlan Garand! Will you shut up? I've had it with you!" Phoebe leaped to her feet, fists clenched at her sides, full bosom heaving.

"Garand?" Richard appeared to be making some connection in his mind. "Anything to do with the Garand freight forwarding firm?" He turned his grey glance on Harlan intently.

"Yes." Harlan's response was stiff, the mocking note gone completely from his voice as he switched his gaze from Phoebe to Richard. He plainly was not inviting any more inquiries into his job, she thought, sitting down.

"You know of him, Richard?" Phoebe asked, frowning at the taller man.

"Well, yes. I'm aware of the firm, at least. We've used it a number of times to make arrangements to ship to Hong Kong and other places in the East. It's a very successful one, I believe, with offices throughout the South Pacific . . ." His fine brow creased momentarily. "Didn't the old man die a couple of years ago? Are you John Garand's son?" he pursued.

Phoebe glanced at Harlan in time to see him respond with a short, swift inclination of his head. The icy eyes slanted a quick look at her as if to see how she was taking this news.

"A *very* successful firm?" she asked with unnatural gentleness.

"I do all right," he said briefly, sipping his drink and watching her over the rim of the glass.

Before she could follow through with her questions, Richard interrupted.

"Phoebe, I want to get something straight here. This man, who has a certain reputation, I might add now that I place him, says you spent the weekend with him." Richard took a breath and Phoebe knew what was coming next. What she didn't know was how to counter the implicit accusation.

"What I'm asking is, did he bother you in any way? You say you were escaping from two would-be rapists. Was there, in fact a third who should be dealt with?" Richard drew himself impressively to his feet, turning to glare accusingly at Harlan. "I am not without influence in this town, Garand. If you've abused Phoebe in any manner, I shall see to it that those two kidnappers aren't the only ones to suffer the full weight of the law!"

"Richard, Mr. Garand gave me shelter and a couple of meals. Nothing more," Phoebe hastened to say clearly, thinking that Richard was behaving as if he were facing a board of directors. Instinctively she tried to soothe the stern expression from his handsome face.

"You're neglecting to mention the fact that we slept together," Harlan contributed with harsh bluntness.

"Phoebe!" Richard turned to face her. "Is that true? Did he force you . . ."

"No! Please Richard, try to understand. It was very cold and there was only one sleeping bag . . ."

"You slept with him willingly?" Richard looked thunderstruck. "My God! What would your brother say! And here you were supposed to be considering my proposal of marriage! How could you even think of allowing yourself to be seduced? Especially if you had only barely escaped being raped a few hours before you met this man! Perhaps your original story was not the whole truth? Perhaps you've thought up some wild story to explain Mr. Garand's presence . . ."

"My brother!" whispered Phoebe, thoroughly stunned. Suddenly Richard's lack of belief in her story no longer mattered at all. "What do you know about my brother?" A terrible suspicion began to crystallize.

Richard looked taken back by her barely voiced question. It was obvious he had hit his stride as the offended party and had no wish to give up the role to her. "I didn't mention the fact that I know your brother because he had warned me not to imply that he and I had ever had any business dealings . . ." he began stiffly.

"What business dealings?" Phoebe cried, leaping to her feet, a white fury burning deep in her breast.

"Your brother designs for us on occasion. He's helped us a great deal with some new pulp machinery. When he found out you were coming to Portland a few months ago to look for a job, he mentioned the fact to me. I instructed our personnel department to keep an eye out for your résumé. I was more than happy to do your brother a favor and give you a job, Phoebe. You've done excellent work for us and . . ."

"What about asking me to marry you?" Phoebe snarled. "Was that part of the favor you were doing for Steve?"

"Of course not! But after I had met you and gotten to know you, I realized that we'd make a good match. Your brother was frankly very pleased. He has already agreed to do some more work for us. You know he only works when he feels like it and we've been extremely lucky to have his cooperation . . ."

"Get out of here!" Phoebe hissed, enraged. Her glittering gaze encompassed both men. "I want you both out of this apartment or I swear to God I'll call the police!" She reached behind her, groped for a weapon, and felt her fingers close around a small dish which had served as an ornament on the end table. She hoisted it threateningly.

"Now, Phoebe," began Harlan, moving toward her even as Richard stepped back toward the door. "Calm down! Behave yourself! Do you want the whole apartment building to hear you?"

"Don't touch me!" she warned, evading his grasp. "You're no better than he is! You gave me no idea who you really were or what you did! I thought you were a nice guy who *worked* for a living!'' She was being horribly unfair, knew it, and couldn't help herself. The feeling of being much abused was too strong to let her think rationally. ''You never told me you owned a huge company and were rich! Like he is!'' She pointed an accusing finger at the hapless Richard who shrank back under it. ''I asked you what you did for a living!''

''Phoebe, put down that dish and listen to me! You're acting like an obnoxious child . . .'' Harlan's hand whipped out, caught her wrist and removed the potential weapon. With equal efficiency, he grasped the other wrist and locked them together in a one-handed grip.

''You're totally irrational at the moment and it's only because you've had an exhausting weekend that I'm not going to turn you over my knee and beat some sense into you! Be grateful! The temptation is almost more than I can resist. Don't worry, Chambers and I are leaving. I think he's got the message that you don't intend to marry him. Now, try to get yourself under control. I'll call you tomorrow evening, understand?'' His hand tightened around her wrists as she struggled furiously.

''I hear you!'' Phoebe gritted. ''Now get out of my apartment!''

Harlan held her an instant longer, seemed about to say something else, and then released her abruptly, striding toward the door where Richard hovered anxiously. A moment later, both men were gone and Phoebe was left alone with her hurt and anger.

She did something she hadn't done even after learning how her brother had sought to buy her a husband the first time. She cried. Ferd moved restlessly in his cage. His limited vocabulary didn't include words of comfort.

chapter five

"This is rather short notice, don't you think, Miss Hampton?" Melvin Waller peered disapprovingly at Phoebe as she sat stiffly on the other side of the desk.

"My reasons for giving only two weeks notice are personal, Mr. Waller," Phoebe replied aloofly. And I certainly don't intend to go into them with you, you old gossip, she thought feelingly. She gave her superior stare for stare and, as usual, won the small contest. There was no way in the world she could stay at Richard's company now. Not after all that had happened. When she had finally dried her eyes, doused her blotchy face in cold water, and fixed herself a small bite to eat last night she had known that leaving her job was the first step that must be taken to regain her pride.

"Miss Hampton, you hold an important position with Chambers Timber. A *management* position . . ." Waller began dubiously. "Your role in data management . . ."

"No one is indispensable, Mr. Waller. Lois can cover for me. She's been involved with the budget figures and the organization matrix. In fact, she would be an excellent candidate for my replacement."

"Chambers Timber may think twice about promoting another woman into management if they make a habit out of only working a few months and then giving notice!" Waller told her snidely.

"Then Chambers Timber had better be very careful if it decides to start discriminating. There are laws now, Mr. Waller. Furthermore, you know as well as I do that my work has been more than satisfactory. Lois Crompton has been with the firm for several years so no one can possibly say she's *flighty*. You would do well to consider her." Phoebe got to her feet. "If you will please see that those papers get to Personnel, I will begin organizing things for my departure." She turned with a small, highly professional smile and walked out of the office. Men!

Phoebe was careful to keep out of any corridors where Richard might be encountered and at noon she escaped to a downtown park to eat a lonely hotdog purchased from one of the many sidewalk vendors. It was overcast, but that seemed normal to Phoebe after having lived in Portland throughout the late winter and early spring. It fit her mood, she thought, indulging herself in another spate of self-pity which lasted until nearly one o'clock. At five minutes to the hour she pulled herself together with great determination and began to make plans for the future. It helped to itemize, categorize and organize, she thought with rueful humor. The logic of the situation came easily. It was the emotional side of the thing which was causing problems. She must, Phoebe told herself, avoid that aspect and choose a course which would cause her the least amount of problems.

The most important and immediate concern, now that she had handed in her resignation, was not to be at home that evening in the event Harlan actually followed through on his promise the night before and called. Of the two men she had thrown out of her apartment last night, Phoebe decided sadly, Harlan was the one who had managed to inflict the greatest degree of hurt—which was, when one stopped to consider, an idiotic state of affairs. She had been prepared never to see the man again and now that she had an excellent reason not to do so, it hurt. It wasn't that he had lied to her exactly, she thought during the bus ride home. He had simply misled her. She remembered with painful clarity the discussions on men from comfortable backgrounds and winced. From what Richard had implied last night, Harlan Garand came from just such a background! Which only made it all the more impossible that he should be genuinely interested in her, she told herself grimly. She had been a novelty, bursting in on his private weekend with a wild story and looking quite different from his normal preference in females and . . .

Why was she dwelling on the subject? Phoebe scolded herself as she opened the door into her snug little apartment. She wasn't being in the least sensible! One minute hating the man because he couldn't possibly be really attracted to her and the next telling herself she wouldn't want him to be!

The well-tailored white suit and snappy little sandals were relegated to the closet as Phoebe slipped into a comfortable western style shirt and denim slacks. She ran a brush through the thick mass of hair which framed the gentle roundness of her face and stared into the mirror with unusually strong feelings of self-dissatisfaction. Round! Everything about her seemed round! Round face, round hair, round figure . . . Well, she wasn't really fat, she reminded herself with a slight resurgence of spirit. It was just this slight tendency toward plumpness . . . The hell with it, she thought and left the apartment feeling generally annoyed with life. She even ignored Ferd's parting remarks.

There was plenty of daylight outside and she knew

that this far north it would last until nearly nine o'clock. Phoebe started walking, not really caring where she was going, some vague notion of finding a place to eat guiding her steps. Several blocks down the street she found a natural foods restaurant and treated herself to a sunflower seed salad and a bowl of yogurt.

Feeling better for the act of self-denial dinner had represented, she continued on down to the theater district and idly read the marquees advertising films. She had never gone to a movie alone before but it was a way of killing the evening and she felt it would be good for her to practice a bit of assertiveness.

When she emerged from the movie house after sitting through two dull features and the cartoon it was after ten o'clock and dark. Going to the movies alone had proven to be a boring experience. It was the sort of activity that needed to be shared to be completely enjoyed, she realized dismally.

The walk home through dark streets didn't seem particularly attractive so she spent another twenty minutes waiting for a bus which finally deposited her two blocks from the apartment building. The shadowy park on one side and the forbidding doorways on the other gave Phoebe a strong impetus to hurry. Unbidden, memories of the kidnapping the previous Friday came back to trouble her. Why had she stayed out after dark? She should have timed the movie and left in the middle so as to be home before nine . . .

She didn't notice the dark figure detach itself from the side of her building and step forward until he loomed directly in front of her, blocking the path.

"I know this is going to sound depressingly like an irate husband interrogating his errant wife, but damn it! Where the hell have you been all evening?" Harlan's unmistakably rich voice came out of the darkness, conveying a high degree of impatience and irritation. In fact, Phoebe realized, he could be described as downright angry.

She glared at him, recovering from the awful start he had given her and snapped peevishly, "Why did you have to scare me to death like that? I nearly screamed!"

"Serves you right! One would think that any reasonably intelligent woman who had been kidnapped only a few days ago would be a little more cautious about being on city streets at night!" Harlan informed her righteously. "Come on, let's go inside. It's been raining off and on and I'm tired of tring to avoid it by standing under that little umbrella your landlady considers an awning!"

Phoebe glanced automatically at his damp hair, gleaming in the streetlight. He was wearing a suede jacket complete with lambswool lining and looked as though he could have just ridden off the range. It had the effect of making him seem more intimidating than ever. He had caught hold of one wrist and was dragging her along in his wake, heading for the front door.

"I do not recall inviting you into my apartment," Phoebe began haughtily as he pulled her down the entrance hall and stabbed the elevator button with a certain viciousness.

"No? I distinctly recall telling you I would be phoning this evening." He turned a menacing look on her. "When I got no answer by eight o'clock I invited myself on over. I thought you might be pulling a childish trick like refusing to answer the phone. When I got here I discovered you had pulled an even more infantile trick: You had disappeared for the evening! I've been waiting for over two hours, Phoebe Hampton, and I am not in a charitable mood. And to think I came over here with the best of intentions!" he concluded disgustedly.

"Really?" she inquired with deep scorn. "What intentions?" The elevator door opened to receive them as if doing the world a favor and Harlan yanked her inside.

"I had planned to offer you a job, of course," he informed her, looking down at her as if she were a little slow mentally.

"How did you know I was in the market for one?" she gritted, feeling abused and not at all sure how to retaliate.

"Didn't you hand in your resignation today? Where's your key?" Silently Phoebe dug it out and handed it to him. He pushed her through the elevator door and down the hall where he unlocked the door, prodded her inside, and closed it behind them. He tossed the key down onto a small table.

"Well? Didn't you?" he insisted, turning to face her.

"How did you know that?" she inquired icily, hands on the curve of her hips. She watched helplessly as he shrugged out of the heavy coat.

"I figured it would be the first action you took." He hung up the coat in her hall closet and started toward the living room. The wicker settee squeaked alarmingly as he threw himself down on it. "Pretty furniture, but I don't think it's going to wear well," he observed, calmly unfastening the top button of his shirt.

"Stop avoiding the issue and tell me how you knew I had resigned!"

Harlan sighed. "I thought you might have done so because it is exactly what I would have done in the circumstances." He regarded her levelly. "There, does that satisfy you?"

How could he know her so well, Phoebe thought furiously!

92

"The answer to your kind offer of a job is no! There! Does that satisfy you?" she retorted, seating herself angrily in the fan chair.

"I never made the offer. I merely pointed out that it had been in my mind to do so when I first arrived this evening. That was two cold, wet hours ago. I am no longer feeling magnanimous," he told her politely.

Phoebe shrugged with a great air of not caring and leaned back in the chair to eye him thoughtfully through narrowed lids. "Then why," she asked with equal politeness, "are you still hanging around?"

"The first reason is that I'm still waiting for an answer to my initial question," he responded coolly.

"The one about where I've been this evening?" she probed with great casualness.

"Precisely."

"You don't really expect me to tell you, do you?" Phoebe felt her self-confidence returning slowly. There were limits, even for people like Harlan Garand! He couldn't force her to tell him what he wanted to know and she was beginning to derive no small pleasure from being able to deny him something!

"I most certainly do," he contradicted. "I didn't spend the past two hours growing increasingly kindhearted."

"It's none of your business."

"Phoebe, either you tell me where you've been or I'll come over there and wring the information out of you. Don't play games with me!" He didn't raise his voice but Phoebe suddenly knew he would do exactly as promised.

"I went out to eat and then I went to a film." She made no effort to keep the resentful tones out of her voice.

"Alone?"

"Yes! The last thing I wanted tonight was an escort!" she flared.

"Still mad at all men, huh?" he smiled slightly, lounging back into the pillows of the settee and regarding her with a superior, mocking expression which did nothing to endear him to her.

"I feel," she pointed out drily, "that I have justifiable cause."

"Phoebe, I don't care what you think of the Third. I know full well your heart isn't broken over him and your pride, which constitutes the only damaged part, will recover. But I want to get one thing straight between us: I never lied to you this weekend!" There was so much intensity in the last few words that Phoebe blinked in astonishment.

"There are different ways of lying," she remarked evenly.

"I'm aware of that fact."

"You misled me."

"I was functioning under the notion that you knew the whole truth about who I was and what I did for a living. I assumed you were playing some game and saw no reason to participate." Harlan watched her closely.

There was a long moment of silence while Phoebe struggled with the knowledge that she wasn't being totally fair.

"You could have told me who you were after you realized I wasn't lying to you," she finally said forcefully, foreseeing the probable end of the discussion and knowing she was only postponing the inevitable apology.

"Come on, honey!" Phoebe told herself to take no notice of the endearment. Harlan was just being casually cajoling. "What was I supposed to do? All I could think about after that creep showed up in the

to get off the subject which implied a potential romance between them. Harlan was only teasing her now, she told herself.

"Yes, as a matter of fact, there was. I didn't mention it yesterday because I wanted to think about it. I also wanted a chance to check out the Third. The last mistake I made was in not telling you I intend to marry you, Phoebe." Harlan spoke simply, his eyes never leaving hers.

Phoebe, making a valiant effort to recover from the shock, stared at him blankly as if he had just announced he was from outer space. Making a strong attempt at rallying herself, she snapped briskly, "You surprise me! I didn't think you would allow yourself to be motivated by misguided notions of masculine honor. You made it perfectly clear at the cabin that you had no intention of being maneuvered into marriage!"

"I refuse to be maneuvered, but that doesn't mean I'm opposed to the whole idea! Phoebe, we got along famously this weekend, in spite of the fact that we were at cross-purposes part of the time. And I need a wife. Dear Aunt Flo is right about that, much as I hate to admit it. Garand Freight Forwarding has been in the family for three generations. It would be a shame to let it go into other hands. There are so few traditions left in this world. I'm thirty-five years old, tired of the singles scene, and tired of having a series of eligible young females paraded in front of me. I want someone I can trust completely, someone who doesn't care much about the social world, someone I can talk to, someone with a sense of humor, someone who's resourceful . . ."

"Brave, loyal and honest! Good grief, Harlan! Please stop or I shall have to get out my old Girl Scout uniform and reread the laws!" Phoebe found herself suddenly convulsed in laughter.

"I am not accustomed to having women go off into gales of merriment at the thought of marriage to me . . ." Harlan began a little roughly, getting abruptly to his feet and striding across the room to where she sat giggling. Determinedly he reached down and hauled her up beside him.

"Really? How many have you proposed to?" Phoebe managed as the outright laughter subsided gradually into a series of chuckles. She had to treat Harlan and his proposal with the humor it deserved, she thought wildly. Otherwise she would probably cry!

"None," he admitted wryly. "You're the first woman I've thought seriously about marrying. I've been quite content with a bachelor existence until recently . . ."

"Until you got lucky and stumbled on an overgrown Girl Scout! Well, Harlan, don't worry. I'm sure the whole thing is only a temporary aberration brought on by feelings of guilt and the fact that you're probably a little sorry for me. In a few days you'll be happily back into the swing of things and the skinny little blonds will start looking very good again! You'll be extremely grateful to me for not taking advantage of your momentary weakness!"

Phoebe removed her glasses to wipe the tears of laughter and some other emotion which she refused to acknowledge from her eyes. "Let me see," she began lightly, replacing the frames with an absent gesture. "I shall have to find the proper wording for refusing your proposal. Perhaps I could use the phrases I was practicing for Richard and never got a chance to try due to an unwarranted interruption at the time! Harlan, I am duly aware of the honor you have extended to me in making me this offer of marriage, but I must regretfully decline . . ."

"Phoebe, my dear, I haven't made you an offer of marriage," Harlan interrupted to point out emphatically. There was a touch of answering humor now in the brilliant gaze he centered on her face and the firm mouth was twisted slightly at the corners.

"I beg your pardon!" Phoebe began with a small grin. "I seem to have misunderstood . . ."

"You did. I never asked you to marry me. I don't intend to ever ask you. That would be inviting the severest form of rejection, as you've just been at pains to demonstrate! My ego couldn't take it. No, honey, I'm *telling* you that we're going to be married. There, that's much simpler, isn't it? No room for arguments, jokes, scenes, etc."

"Harlan, what's the matter with you?" Phoebe demanded, laughter fading rapidly from her voice as she caught the determination in his. She peered up at him speculatively. "It's not in character for someone like you to want to marry someone like me. If you're really looking for all those admirable characteristics I'm sure you'll find them in a woman from your own world. One who's small and blond in the bargain! I'm sure your aunt could help you locate a charming creature who will suit the role of Mrs. Harlan Garand to perfection!"

"What do you know of my world, Phoebe? There's a great deal you don't know about me or what I want out of life, but you'll learn. I have great faith in your native intelligence!" Harlan smiled almost gently, removed her glasses delicately and, placing them down carefully, pulled her close into a tight embrace.

Despite the gentleness of his voice, there was nothing soft about Harlan's kiss. It was as if he took up the lovemaking where he had left off on Saturday night, Phoebe thought frantically, feeling her response rise almost immediately to meet his. How could he demand

99

and receive such instant reciprocation when her brain was clearly calling for caution from her body? Had she no self-control left at all when it came to this man? She must! Her future happiness depended on not surrendering completely, Phoebe lectured herself, even while her lips softened beneath his and her mouth opened to receive the warmth of him. His arms tightened as he felt her weakening and Harlan deliberately pursued his advantage.

Telling herself she could retreat and reestablish her barricades later, Phoebe surrendered to the onslaught. Even in his present mood of conquering, dominating male, Harlan's arms held more satisfaction than Phoebe had ever before known. For the first time in her life she was dealing with a man who was able and willing to use his strength and his sexual technique when words failed to get him what he wanted. The power of it was overwhelming.

Sensing her crumbling resistance, Harlan shifted his hold, letting strong hands mold her body against his until she was fully aware of the male need growing in him. His mouth left hers to nibble delicately at the tip of her ear and Phoebe found herself clinging helplessly to him, the only steady object in a room which had begun to whirl dangerously. The tighter she clung, the more Harlan consolidated his attack, taking advantage of every weakness, every tiny retreat, seeming to revel in each new surrender. It wasn't until Phoebe felt her feet leave the floor as Harlan swung her into his arms that she came back to some vague sense of reality.

"Harlan!" she gasped, her head spinning as she was cradled against his chest. Dimly she was aware of the fact that he was striding down the hall to her bedroom apparently oblivious to the weight in his arms. The romantic side of her nature was thrusting fiercely to the fore, pointing out that he was treating her exactly as if she really were a tiny, fragile blond. The practical streak was at a loss to know how to stop him.

"Harlan, wait," she tried feebly.

"Quiet, sweetheart," he ordered softly, huskily, finding the door to her bedroom and entering as if he had every right. "I forgot to mention one other reason why I intend to marry you," he whispered, dumping her lightly on the bed and following immediately, sprawling across her bed with casual disregard. "I find you irresistible, my cuddly little Phoebe. You fill my hands so sweetly with your softness and I find I want more and more of you. As my intentions are quite honorable, I fail to see why I should bother trying to restrain myself! Besides," he grinned wickedly down at her, "I have the distinct impression I can make you do anything I want when you're in my arms. The temptation to exercise that kind of power is more than I can withstand!" He lowered his lips deliberately to the hollow of her throat. "And I have an urgent need to find out what you're like when you let yourself go completely, my Phoebe!" His hand moved along the curve of her hip, into the dip of her waist, and on up to rest beneath the heaviness of one breast. His thumb glided across the tip, exciting the nipple through the layers of fabric.

Phoebe closed her eyes, trying desperately to reason through a situation that was not at all reasonable. Harlan didn't, *couldn't* really want her—not as a wife, not forever! She was merely something new in his world. A woman who represented a change of pace, but not one of the type he admitted admiring! His mad proposal was born out of his feelings of guilt, she told herself. He must be given time to think, to reconsider. And he must do it before he had made love to her completely! She couldn't bear to have him change his mind afterward!

"Harlan, listen to me!" Phoebe begged, trying futilely to twist out from under the length of his hard body. "You haven't done anything right tonight!" The last was uttered in a tone of outraged despair and it stopped him cold.

Harlan lifted his head and simply stared down at her. Phoebe returned the look, heart in her mouth.

"Would you mind explaining that last remark?" he inquired deliberately, not moving. One red brow crooked upward warningly.

Phoebe licked a dry lip, gathering her thoughts, trying to marshal them into arguments which would buy her what her physical strength never could—time.

"Harlan, I don't believe for a moment that you really mean to marry me."

"No?" There was a dangerous seasoning of steel in the deep voice.

"No," Phoebe responded with growing firmness. "I told you, I think you're acting out of some misguided idea that you owe me something. Or perhaps I'm different enough from your normal choice in women to intrigue you for a short time. But if you are the least serious, you owe me a lot more than what you've seen fit to give me tonight!"

"What the hell is that supposed to mean?" he growled, the hand on her breast tightening.

"It means that just because I don't happen to be beautiful and blond and thin, I don't want to be treated that way by the man who says he wants to marry me!" she whispered nervously. "Look at it from my point of view, Harlan," she begged. "You accost me on my way home tonight, inform me that you're going to marry me for all sorts of wholesome reasons, and then pick me up and carry me off to the bedroom—my *own* bedroom, I might add, as if you had every right in the world! Even you have to admit that's rushing things somewhat! A woman deserves more than that from a prospective husband!" Phoebe concluded feelingly.

"What more does she deserve?" Harlan asked menacingly.

"Some romance, for heavens sake!" Phoebe was rapidly taking heart from her own words, her spirit surfacing as she realized how just her cause was. "I'll bet you never acted this way with any of your little blonds!"

"I never planned to marry any of them!" Harlan snapped, sounding mightily aggrieved. "I thought you were a woman of common sense! What do you want with all those dumb games?"

"That goes to show how little you know about me!" she shot back. "I want to be romanced! To be courted!"

"As I see it," Harlan continued in almost conversational tones, "I now have two options open. I can revert back to my recently interrupted attempt at seduction. Which attempt, I believe, would be entirely successful. On the other hand, I could try and convince you that I'm well aware of what I'm doing by marrying you."

Phoebe drew a careful breath. "There is," she said delicately, "another alternative you might consider."

"Which is?" he asked with mild interest.

"You could," she said softly, "court me."

"Court you?" he repeated, obviously surprised. "Phoebe, I told you at the cabin that I don't see myself as able to conduct a very restrained sort of courtship, which is probably the type you have in mind!"

"Harlan, all I want is a little time. Time for you to make certain of your feelings and time for me to understand mine. Is that too much to ask? I want to be certain there's really love between us!"

Harlan glared down at her for a long moment. Then he appeared to come to a decision. "I will," he announced with the attitude of one who is making a huge concession, "court you until the end of the Rose Festival." His expression dared her to throw out a counter offer.

"The Rose Festival ends somewhere in the middle of June, doesn't it?" Phoebe frowned, trying to recall the publicity she had seen on the annual event.

"It ends on the tenth of June. We'll be married no later than the eleventh," he stated uncompromisingly.

"But, Harlan! That's only three weeks away!" Phoebe wailed.

"Take your pick: Three days from now or three weeks from now."

"I promise to consider the offer very seriously over the next three weeks," Phoebe said with fake calm.

"Don't look too smug, Phoebe," he warned mockingly. "You've asked for a courtship and you'll get it. But it will be run by my rules!"

chapter six

The yellow roses were waiting outside her door the next morning. Phoebe discovered them as she prepared to leave for work. She immediately assumed the florist had made a delivery error and was about to take them down to the manager's office when she noticed the card addressed to herself. With a funny twinge of elation, she ripped it open and read the brief note inside. It was scrawled in a huge, lazy hand which she knew instantly belonged to Harlan and it read simply "To match your bedspread." Wryly, Phoebe smiled and remembered once again how at home the man had made himself in her bedroom the previous evening. A further almost indecipherable line told her to be ready for dinner at seven. Typical arrogance, she told herself, inserting the card back into the envelope and carrying the flowers inside the apartment. He hadn't even signed the note! The assumption that there were no other men in her life who might be sending yellow roses was as annoying as it was accurate.

"Look at these, Ferd. Harlan's first effort at courtship. What do you think?" Phoebe extended the roses toward the cage and the bird eyed them thoughtfully for a moment and then pronounced his verdict:

"Fee, fie, fo, fum . . ."

"Yes, yes, I know," she interrupted him. "You smell the blood of an Oregonian. It's a pity we haven't had more time to work on your language lessons!"

At ten o'clock Phoebe received a phone call in her office from Richard's secretary. She was requested to appear in the managing director's office in fifteen minutes. Phoebe knew the curtness of the instruction was a little something extra added by Janice Taylor, the secretary. Poor Janice would have given her right arm to be dating Richard, Phoebe thought with a sigh. She wondered if she ought to drop a hint or two in the other girl's ear. She could have told the blond, for instance, that Richard needed someone more conservative looking for his wife. Someone who could project refined elegance, not a showgirl level of beauty. Phoebe had often wondered how she had qualified for Richard's consideration herself, feeling she fell far short of the elegant look or even the showgirl look! Well, now she knew. Was she never to be free of her brother's influence?

"Go right on in, Miss Hampton," Janice remarked coolly, not even bothering to glance up from her typing. Phoebe studied the California-look hairdo, the silk blouse opened one button too far and the slightly pouting cast of the artfully colored lips and almost said something. Then she changed her mind and walked into Richard's office without a word. She did not anticipate a pleasant interview.

Richard rose as soon as she entered the room and Phoebe smiled politely, taking the chair he indicated.

"Hello, Phoebe. Sorry to pull you away from your work but I felt we should talk. I, uh, understand from Personnel that you've handed in your resignation?" He spoke hesitantly, the grey eyes not quite focusing on her.

"That's right. I think it would be a bit awkward for me to stay on after what happened Sunday night, don't you?" Phoebe was amazed by the calm sound of her own voice.

"Phoebe, I wish you would reconsider. You've done an excellent job here and have become a valuable member of the staff in only a few months." He paused. "I also want you to know that I'm sorry for not believing your story about being kidnapped. I talked to the police this morning and have let my acquaintances on the force know how strongly I feel about them finding the other man who was in that truck . . ."

"Thank you, Richard," she said politely, "I'm sure they'll do their best. As for filling the position I'm vacating, well, perhaps there is someone else's sister looking for a job . . ." Instantly, Phoebe wished she hadn't been so blatantly rude. Richard didn't deserve that. He couldn't help the way he behaved. He was a product of his environment.

"Phoebe, please! As much as I value your brother's genius and his contribution to this company, that doesn't mean I would have given you a position of genuine responsibility unless you were properly qualified! One doesn't staff a firm of this size with incompetents just to please certain people!"

Phoebe winced. "Oh, Richard, let's not discuss this any more. The truth of the matter is, I wasn't going to marry you regardless so the result is the same as far as our relationship goes . . ."

"No, it's not the same! I have my pride, too, you see. I want to make it clear that just as I wouldn't have hired you if I hadn't been impressed by your credentials in information and data management, I wouldn't have asked you to marry me if I hadn't thought you'd make a good wife! Please believe me. Your brother's intelligence and wealth would be an asset to any family in this day and age, but I wouldn't have married you just to obtain a closer connection with him! I truly wanted to marry you, Phoebe." He looked directly at her now, apparently intent on convincing her of the basic integrity of his intentions. "You . . . you're different," he added lamely.

"Different?" she queried, intrigued by this new, hesitant side of a man who had always seemed so logical, deliberate, and controlled.

"You're nice to be with. I can talk to you and you don't expect me to . . . to carry out the playboy role, if you know what I mean?" He looked away again, focusing his gaze out the window toward the snow covered peak of Mount Hood in the distance.

"I see." Phoebe smiled with a measure of understanding. "I hadn't realized how you felt pressured by your image."

"That's just it! With you I don't feel that way!" Richard smiled ruefully. "I can relax with you."

"But I could never have fallen in love with you, Richard," she said gently.

"Why not? You seemed to enjoy going out with me."

"Dating you was one thing. I did enjoy your company. Very much. But I don't think we would have been happy together for the rest of our lives. You need someone beautiful who won't mind mixing continuously in the crowd you move with. I'm not that woman, Richard."

"You could have adapted, Phoebe . . ."

"I might have been able to adapt but I don't want to adapt. There's a huge difference. Now if you want to meet someone who has both the looks and the willingness to be your wife and the social ornament you need, I suggest you step out that door and introduce yourself to your secretary!"

"Janice!" Richard looked stunned.

"She's head over heels in love with you, Richard.

Didn't you ever guess?''

"No, I . . ."

"Oh, you might have to guide her along the ways of society, but I guarantee she'll be a willing learner! In fact, she'd make a career out of being your wife!"

"But Janice is beautiful! She'd expect so much . . ." Richard faltered, realizing he'd made an unforgivable blunder.

"Whereas us homely types don't pressure a man unduly?" Phoebe got to her feet with great dignity and even managed a distant smile. "Goodbye, Richard."

She swung through the door and pulled it closed with unnatural softness behind her. What had she ever seen in that man! For an instant she stood regarding the hurt look in Janice Taylor's attractive brown eyes and then she stepped over to the desk and leaned down confidentially.

"He's all yours, Janice. Want some advice?"

"What are you talking about, Miss Hampton?" Janice's carefully made-up face was unable to hide the degree of surprise she was experiencing at this unexpected assault from the sedate Phoebe Hampton.

"I'm talking about buttoning that blouse," Phoebe reached over and did it for her before the other girl could react. "Go wash off some of that makeup. You scare him. And get that hair back out of your face. You'll need a more refined image to catch Richard. Remember, you have to sell yourself to his mother and sister, as well! The last tip is, don't make him feel that he's expected to be a super stud. Let him do the talking. He loves to talk about himself!"

"Miss Hampton!" Janice looked fascinated.

"One more thing. Do you play tennis?"

Suddenly Janice Taylor grinned. "No, but I'm willing to learn!"

"Then you've got it made. I was never ready to make the supreme sacrifice. Not the athletic type, I guess. Which only goes to show that I wasn't really in love with the man, doesn't it?" Phoebe winked and walked out the door.

Harlan's unmistakable knock sounded on Phoebe's door at five minutes to seven that evening and she went to answer, having serious second thoughts about the whole matter but unable to think of a way out. It wasn't as if, she told herself, there was a great deal of choice in the matter. While she wasn't quite sure what he would have done if she hadn't been waiting for him, she knew Harlan well enough now to know ther would have been inescapable reprisals. Besides, this strange whim of his had to end soon, she thought glumly. Why shouldn't she take advantage of the situation to enjoy the excitement of his company while she could? Or as long as she could keep him out of her bed, at any rate! That way, Phoebe knew with a strong sense of certainty, lay pain. She would never, ever be able to put Harlan Garand out of her mind if she once allowed him to possess her. And that's what making love with him would be, Phoebe thought. An act of possession on his part, an act of surrender on hers. Not a very modern approach to the subject!

"Good evening," she greeted him very properly, opening the door to reveal Harlan dressed in an evening jacket. At once she was very glad she had dressed for the occasion.

"You didn't mention where we would be dining so I hope this is suitable?" She indicated the soft, clinging green gown, its halter top displaying a tantalizing amount of smooth, erect back. Her hair had been brushed into a sleek cape which was parted in the middle and curled softly inward at the ends. Small evening

110

sandals completed the outfit, together with a tiny gold bracelet.

"You look perfect," Harlan smiled, moving his elegantly covered shoulders through the door. "Soft and rounded and incredibly sexy!"

"Sexy!" Phoebe stared at him, astounded. It was not a term which had often been applied to her before!

"Yes. Sexy!" Without another word, he stepped toward her and planted a quick, proprietary kiss on her surprised lips. "The contrast between my Phoebe dressed like this and my Phoebe in jeans is delightful."

"Harlan, you're embarrassing me! If you're going to spend the evening talking like this . . ." Phoebe broke off, very flustered.

"I have lots of things to discuss tonight. After all, this is the first day of the courtship!"

"You're really going to go through with it?" she asked dubiously, one brow climbing over the top of the rounded frames of her glasses.

"Naturally. Did you get the flowers?" He glanced around the room, saw the yellow roses displayed prominently on the table by the window and looked enormously pleased with himself.

"They're lovely. Thank you very much," Phoebe smiled politely, wanting to tease him about the sheer male ego he was exposing, but not quite daring.

He nodded. "Good. Let's go, then. Better bring a wrap, it could get chilly later."

"Yes, Harlan."

"That's what I like to hear," he told her approvingly, holding the door as she swept through, into the hallway.

"Enjoy it while you can. You won't hear such words very often!" she informed him with a regal lift to her chin. Phoebe ignored his chuckle.

The restaurant he had chosen was terribly romantic,

she decided. Candlelight, snowy white linen, silver and crystal, and an emphasis on French cooking. Phoebe glanced around as Harlan held her chair and smiled sweetly.

"Roses in the morning, candlelight and wine at night. Do you do a lot of courting, Harlan?" she inquired demurely, taking the seat which left her facing the stone wall—and Harlan. He obviously intended no distractions, she thought, realizing he knew quite well what he was doing when he seated her.

"No, darling, a lot of seduction," he informed her easily, settling into the large chair opposite her.

The tips of Phoebe's small ears burned as she felt the hovering maitre d' stifle a smile.

"Harlan!" she snapped, brows coming together reprovingly.

"You asked for it, honey," he told her carelessly, accepting the wine list and the menu. "Now, I promised myself I'd try very hard tonight, so don't provoke me," he instructed as the man disappeared.

Phoebe sighed. "Yes, Harlan. I wouldn't want to put a strain on your good manners or your good intentions!"

"That's right. Now let's choose dinner so we can get on with tonight's discussion!"

"You've got the evening completely programmed?" she demanded, feeling her lips twitch in an effort to keep from smiling.

"I've got the next three weeks planned!" he informed her grandly. "You wanted a courtship, you'll get it!"

What have I let myself in for, Phoebe wondered, unable to ignore the excitement and tension between herself and Harlan. The romance might come to a bad end, but at least it wasn't going to be dull as it had been with Richard!

With the arrival of the first course and a bottle of California Sauvignon Blanc Harlan plunged into the topic of the evening.

"Courtship," he began impressively, "is supposed to be a time when two people discover the likes and dislikes of the other."

"You've been reading up on the subject?"

"I've wracked my brain trying to figure out a way of occupying the next several evenings other than making love to you. Discussing likes and dislikes seems an ideal beginning!"

"I see," Phoebe nearly choked on her salad.

"Now. Do you or don't you like children?"

"My own or someone else's?" Phoebe asked, beginning to get into the spirit of the thing.

"Don't be flippant," Harlan ordered, grinning. "We are discussing the heir to the Garand Freight Forwarding business!"

"If my husband was absolutely convinced he wanted a child or two and if he was certain in his own mind that he would make a good father, I would consider becoming a mother."

"Don't be so cautious, Phoebe! It's obvious you were born to be a mother!" Harlan proclaimed, refilling her wine glass.

"Is it? I have that maternal look?" she asked crisply, not very happy with his comment.

"You have a loving look," he corrected mildly, catching her eye and smiling blandly. "You are one of those women designed by nature to create a home."

"What makes you such an expert?"

"Instinct."

"Well, your instinct is wrong this time, Harlan. I enjoy my career and don't see myself tied to a kitchen sink!"

"Ah, that's where we differ! Now I picture you barefoot, pregnant and most definitely confined to the kitchen!"

"Harlan Garand! Quit teasing me or I'll take myself home right this minute!" Phoebe was torn between laughter and indignation. Laughter won.

"That's better," he nodded approvingly.

"I'll make a deal with you," Phoebe offered brightly. "You agree to split the child-caring duties and spend lots of time with your heirs and I'll agree to have one or two of the little darlings. Fair enough?"

"Sounds reasonable," he nodded. "Maybe we should go a step farther and split the breadwinning, too."

"I'll run half of Garand Freight Forwarding and you'll run the other half?" Phoebe suggested.

"I'm not saying I'll give up my position as president," he corrected, "but I expect we could find you a position somewhere in the firm."

"Sounds like a clear case of nepotism."

"What's the point of running your own company if you can't do as you wish?"

Phoebe laughed outright, the happy sound turning the heads of a few amused diners nearby.

"I'm not sure I like the idea of taking orders from you all day long!" she protested.

"But I'm so good at giving them!" he grinned back.

"I'll just bet you are! I still haven't forgotten those fish! No, I think I'll maintain a separate career."

"Independent little creature, aren't you? Did the Third know what he was letting himself in for when he asked you to marry him?" Harlan asked interestedly.

"Oh, I found out this morning what my real attraction was," Phoebe chuckled, beginning to relax with he second glass of wine.

"You saw Chambers today?" Harlan asked, some of

the humor fading from his eyes. He watched her obliquely, waiting for her response.

"Yes, he'd just discovered I'd turned in my resignation and wanted to assure me that I didn't have to go to such lengths. He said that I had been an asset to the company and that his offer of marriage had been genuine. Prompted by the fact that he could talk to me," Phoebe confided.

"Talk to you? What the hell did he mean by that?"

"I don't make him feel pressured into being a playboy type," Phoebe smiled.

"I see. Well, I don't think there's any more need for you to discuss your past relationship with the man, Phoebe. It's finished. I don't want you to get into a position where you start feeling sorry for him!" Harlan was all business now, lecturing her firmly across the table.

"Some of the romance is going out of my evening, Harlan," she noted drily.

"Is it? That's all right, courtship is also an opportunity for the male to assert his right as head of the new family!"

"Courtship," Phoebe pointed out determinedly, "is an opportunity for the female to change her mind and get out of a situation that doesn't look promising!"

"It's a time when said female had better practice a little feminine subservience or risk getting paddled in front of God and the maitre d'!"

"No more romance tonight?" Phoebe pouted. "How depressing! And I had such high hopes this morning after the roses arrrived! But, I suppose it's typical for the male to resort to threats of physical violence when he can't get what he wants by intelligent argument . . ."

"I can get what I want any time I choose," Harlan told her with mocking menace, "by taking you to bed and we both know it. If you wish me to continue with the other aspects of courtship such as flowers and conversation, you had better heed my wishes in such matters as Richard Elton Chambers III. To be blunt, I don't want you seeing him in anything other than a business sense!''

Phoebe burst out laughing. "Poor Harlan! You feel so self-sacrificing don't you?''

"I consider I'm being extremely generous," yes," he agreed readily, his expression lightening as he studied her laughing face. "It's not every woman I'd go through a courtship for!''

Abruptly Harlan's gaze shifted to a point past her left shoulder.

"Friend of yours?" he asked and Phoebe turned to see Julie Chambers advancing on them. Beautiful, thin, blond Julie. Phoebe could have wished for anyone else at that particular moment.

"Phoebe! How are you, dear?" Richard told me what happened on Friday. How ghastly for you! Thank heavens you're all right. You must have been absolutely terrified!''

"I was, Julie," Phoebe acknowledged her with a polite smile, knowing now that she and Richard's sister could never have been friends. "But everything's all right now. The police have one of the characters, thanks to Harlan here, and it's probably only a matter of time before they pick up the other one. Your brother has instructed them to put forth their best efforts," she added with a touch of mockery. She turned in her seat and made introductions.

"How do you do, Miss Chambers," Harlan said calmly, eyeing the shimmering length of the attractive girl who seemed to preen under his regard.

"Harlan Spencer Garand? Of the Garand firm? I

116

believe my brother has mentioned you . . ."

Phoebe watched the other woman's light blue eyes clash with Harlan's brilliant gaze and felt such a wave of jealousy that she had to exercise considerable self-control just to stay in her seat. Some primitive reaction was trying to drive her to her feet to confront this other woman who was so obviously what Harlan wanted. Or was what he'd want again after he'd gotten over his temporary interest in Phoebe!

"Won't you sit down, Miss Chambers?" Harlan invited cordially, apparently oblivious to the flash of pain Phoebe knew had crossed her face. What was the matter with her? Wasn't it better to let Harlan find out the truth about himself quickly rather than a couple of weeks from now?

"You and Phoebe are out celebrating the lucky escape?" Julie hazarded, glancing from one to the other. She knows, Phoebe thought. Those malicious little blue eyes see everything. And Richard has probably already told her . . .

"Phoebe and I are going to be married," Harlan corrected. "In a way, though, I suppose we ought to be celebrating her escape too. If she hadn't had the courage to free herself I would never have met her!" He smiled into Phoebe's eyes and she warmed instantly. He was being very kind, she thought.

"Married!" Julie turned toward Phoebe. "You and Richard are through, then? Permanently?" She seemed intently interested in Phoebe's answer. Probably relieved I'm freeing her brother for a more suitable marriage, Phoebe decided and nodded.

"I see." The other girl turned a cool gaze back to Harlan. "Exactly how did the two of you meet? It's all quite sudden, isn't it?"

"Well, just between the three of us," Harlan began in

a suspiciously confiding tone, "there wasn't much choice. I mean, after all, Phoebe wound up spending the weekend with me, you know!"

"Harlan!" Phoebe's poor protest was lost in Julie's outright laughter.

"You mean you're marrying the girl because you've compromised her? Oh, Harlan! What a marvelous joke! Wait until I tell my date!" Julie nodded toward the far corner of the room where a man was seated alone, staring across at them. "This is great! Everyone's going to love the story!"

"Julie, please," Phoebe began, glaring at Harlan who simply smiled benignly.

"My compliments, Phoebe," Julie smiled falsely. "You got a much better catch than Richard would have been. I mean, everyone knows the Garand firm is a very successful one! I'm sure Harlan here is much wealthier than my brother! And to think you trapped him into marriage! It's the best story I've heard in ages!" She got to her feet, smiling down at Harlan. "Please excuse me now, I really can't keep this one to myself any longer!" She lifted perfectly manicured nails in a graceful gesture of farewell and moved off.

"Now we can return to our conversation in peace," Harlan announced contentedly, picking up his knife and engaging his steak in battle.

"Harlan Garand! How could you! Of all the mean, cruel, malicious things to do to a woman . . ." Phoebe began, barely able to speak with the intensity of her emotion.

"Cruel? I wasn't cruel to her!" Harlan protested, looking incredibly innocent.

"Not her! Me! The woman you claim you want to marry! How dare you embarrass me by telling her you're marrying me because I spent the weekend with you!"

"You're a fetching sight when you're angry, honey, but you aren't doing your digestion any good. Why don't you calm down and have another glass of wine? I got rid of her, didn't I?"

"No, thank you! I would prefer to go home!" She ignored his last comment.

"But I'm not ready to take you home. Simmer down and stop looking at me with that Ferd expression! I didn't bring any birdseed along. Or is that part of the courting ritual I don't know about?"

For a long moment Phoebe locked wills with him across the white linen tablecloth and then her sense of humor got the better of her.

"Harlan, you're absolutely impossible!" she groaned, reaching for her wine glass.

"I'm a good dancer, though," he told her brightly. "Finish your dinner and I'll show you!"

"How come," Phoebe inquired an hour later as Harlan led her back to the small table in the lounge, "we only dance the slow dances?"

"You forget. I'm an older man," he grinned down at her. "Besides, I'm only concerned with the dances which give me an excuse to hold you. You're such a pleasant armful, sweetheart!" He reached out and lifted her hand. "Tomorrow we should go shopping for a ring. I'll meet you on your lunch hour and we can go to the jeweler's . . ."

"Harlan . . ." Phoebe began worriedly. A ring would make the whole unbelievable situation too real. It might make everything hurt too much when it all ended!

"No arguments, honey. I'm anxious to get my mark of ownership on you. The old male ego at work, you understand."

Phoebe flushed.

119

"If I could, I'd be buying leg irons tomorrow and a matching slave collar," Harlan continued, pinning her beneath his glittering look.

"What's the matter?" Phoebe demanded, rallying her forces bravely to confront the very masculine expression he was wearing. "Don't you trust your own abilities to keep me where you want me?"

"Not entirely. At least, not yet." Harlan regarded her deliberately for a moment. "Once you're mine completely and I've wrung all the promises and words out of you that I want to hear, I'll feel more confident. This courtship . . ."

"You promised me the courtship," Phoebe broke in hurriedly, anxious to keep him from changing his mind. It was true, he hadn't actually guaranteed not to take her to bed during the next three weeks but she had the impression that they shared a certain understanding on the subject. It was a delicate tightrope that Phoebe was walking and she knew it. The seductive danger lay all around her and if she had any sense she'd run a hundred miles in the opposite direction. But somehow she couldn't bring herself to deny her own desire to bask in the magic of his attention as long as possible. But she must manage it without letting herself get too badly hurt. The experience of being courted by Harlan Spencer Garand was worth a certain amount of pain, but not the deluge which would be hers if she gave herself to him completely.

"You don't need to remind me of what I got talked into last night! I shouldn't have let you do it. I know I shouldn't!" Harlan sighed ruefully. "If I had any sense I would drive you home right now, take what is mine, and put an end to this nonsense!"

Phoebe smiled tremulously, aware of the danger in his present mood.

"Think how noble you're going to feel in the morning if you stick by your promise tonight!" she suggested hopefully.

"I'm going to feel like a fool in the morning," he corrected. "Let's dance!"

Later that night, Phoebe started toward her bedroom, her hands at work on the fastening of her gown as she moved. She was in the process of freeing herself from the bodice when she realized the bedroom window was wide open. It brought her to a halt. A strange feeling of something not being quite right coursed down her spine in a wave. That window had been closed when she left for the evening. Had someone entered the apartment? She remembered the convenient fire escape near the window. But what would anyone want . . .

Without another thought, Phoebe backed out of the room, clutching the front of the gown to her throat and raced to the door. Flinging it open she spotted Harlan instantly as he leaned casually against the wall waiting for the elevator.

Without another thought, Phoebe backed out of the room, clutching the front of the gown to her throat and raced to the door. Flinging it open she spotted Harlan instantly as he leaned casually against the wall waiting for the elevator.

"Phoebe! What's wrong!" he demanded, striding forward immediately and grasping her shoulders in a painful grip.

"I think," she began, breathing deeply in an effort to bring her emotions under control, "that someone has been in my apartment while we were out! Oh, Harlan that awful little man said his friend Max would get me! Do you think . . . ?"

chapter seven

"You're absolutely certain that window was closed when we left this evening, honey?" Harlan asked for the third time as they stood in the living room trying to make sense out of the incident. A rapid tour of the small apartment had revealed nothing missing and if there had been any footprints on the fire escape the evening rain had washed them away.

"As sure as I can be, Harlan. I suppose there's a possibility I forgot to close it, but . . ." Phoebe's voice trailed off thoughtfully. She knew she had closed that window!

"If only Ferd could talk," Harlan commented.

"Fee, fie, fo, fum," began Ferd obligingly, hopping from one perch to another, his beady eyes on the two humans.

"Shut up, Ferd," Phoebe said absently. She had refastened the gown and kicked off the sandals. Moving across to the fan chair she sat down and looked up at Harlan consideringly.

"I think we have to go on the assumption I was wrong," she began wearily. "We certainly can't call the police on such flimsy evidence!"

"Still in the morning I think I'll give that detective we spoke to a call and let him know what happened. Just in case. He can make what he wants to out of it." Harlan studied her silently for a moment and then stepped in front of her, leaning down to take one of her hands in his and tug Phoebe to her feet.

"Come on, honey, it's getting late and we both have to be at work in the morning."

"Goodnight again," Phoebe smiled. "And thanks for looking through the apartment with me. Sorry to have sounded so panicked a few minutes ago."

"I can't even imagine you in a real panic, Phoebe," he grinned. "But there's no reason for you to have to spend the evenings being nervous, either. Get some things together and I'll take you somewhere else to spend the night."

"There's no need for that," she protested quickly, a sudden suspicion forming in her mind.

"Of course, there's a need for it! I'm not going to leave you here alone and that's final! You'd lie awake all night wondering if somebody was going to come through that window! Even worse, I'd be worrying about the same thing! So come along now, there's a good girl, and get whatever you'll need for tomorrow . . ."

"Harlan, I'm not going with you!" Phoebe dug her toes into the rug beneath her feet and glared at him.

"Why not?" he inquired, lifting an eyebrow curiously. "Ah! Wait a second, you think I'm going to take you to my place, right?"

"Well?" she challenged. "Isn't that what you have in mind?"

"If it is?"

"Then you can forget it! You promised me a court-ship!" Phoebe concluded on a wail.

"And you think that if I take you home with me you won't get your courtship?"

"I would probably," she said with grand dignity, "never see another yellow rose from you again!"

"Maybe you'd have something much better than roses," he suggested, blue eyes glinting.

"What could be better than yellow roses in the morning?" she retorted, trying to keep her words flippant. She would not go home with him tonight!

"How about me in the morning?" he asked curiously.

"It wouldn't be the same," she informed him, shaking her head firmly.

"I'm crushed. But that doesn't change matters. You're still not spending the night here."

"I won't spend it with you, either!"

"No, I concede defeat for tonight. I'm taking you to Aunt Flo's. There, does that satisfy you?"

"Your aunt's? But it's midnight! We can't go barging in on her at this hour! She doesn't even know me!" Phoebe said quickly, thinking of a poor, elderly soul being dragged out of her bed by an inconsiderate nephew and having a strange woman thrust on her.

"I told her all about you this morning. Called her from the office before I even looked at the mail my secretary had opened for me! She's dying to meet you and the drama of the whole thing tonight will charm her enormously. Now stop making difficulties and pack a nightie or whatever it is women pack when they go visiting. Don't forget your toothbrush!"

Phoebe surrendered. It was late, she was tired, and finding that window open had been an unnerving experience. She packed her nightie and a toothbrush and then walked back out into the living room where Harlan was thumbing idly through a magazine.

"Can I bring Ferd?" she asked. "He won't like being left alone overnight again so soon and there's no telling what sort of tantrum he might decide to throw."

"Bring Ferd, by all means. He'll get along famously with Aunt Flo. Did you pack something to wear into the office tomorrow?" Harlan indicated the small bag in Phoebe's hand.

She nodded. "Yes, but I'm not sure the situation is worth all this, Harlan. I mean chances are I did leave that window open and . . ."

"I'm not going to have you fretting over it, honey," he announced, getting to his feet and tossing the magazine aside. "Get the bird and whatever he needs. I'll take your bag."

A few minutes later Phoebe found herself seated in the front seat of Harlan's Jaguar, Ferd's cage on her lap. She had put the cover over it, but the bird could be heard muttering to himself inside. It was obvious he didn't think very much of being hustled off in the middle of the night.

"I'm going to stop by my place and pick up Jinx and a few other items," Harlan informed her blandly as he put the car in gear and pulled neatly out of the parking slot in front of the apartment house.

"I see."

"Still think I'm going to drag you off to my bed and make wild, passionate love to you tonight?" he inquired interestedly, flashing her a slanting glance.

"Just concerned about losing my morning roses, as I mentioned earlier," she told him airily, wondering what it would be like to have him do exactly as he had suggested. What would one night of wild, passionate love with Harlan be worth? A lifetime of regret? A lifetime of memories? Phoebe fixed her gaze firmly out the window at the dark streets slipping past the luxurious Jag.

"My God! I can see I've spoiled you already! I shall have to place a permanent order for yellow roses with the florist!" Harlan drove out of the downtown area and began the climb into the nearby hills where the older and wealthier residential areas were to be found. She should have guessed, Phoebe told herself as she caught sight of some of the elegant homes slumbering in the light of streetlamps. Harlan didn't appear to be lacking materially.

Some time later he angled off the road onto a winding drive which led to a surprisingly modern-looking home nestled in among the firs. Phoebe surveyed the sleek lines of wood and glass appraisingly.

"Like it?" Harlan smiled, watching her face carefully.

"I suppose I was expecting something older in this neighborhood. It's lovely, Harlan. Did you have it specially built?" Phoebe glanced at him, wondering why he had an almost anxious look on his lean features. Was he really concerned that she should like his home?

"Yes, last year, in fact. After I had settled down to being a businessman at last."

"When did you take over your father's firm?" Phoebe asked, remembering something Richard had said on Sunday night about a John Garand.

"Two years ago," Harlan replied shortly.

"You don't sound as if it was your goal in life," Phoebe heard herself say gently, looking at him in the glow of the car's interior lighting system.

"It wasn't at the time. But strangely enough I've come to enjoy it. Being in charge has its advantages! I'm satisfied with my work and that's why I've started thinking about complying with family tradition and producing an heir," he grinned across at her.

"You're willing to force some other young man into the business on the grounds that he'll come to enjoy it, too?" Phoebe lifted one brow aloofly.

"Maybe we'll have a daughter who will turn out to be a natural business leader!"

Phobe laughed at that. "And here I was thinking you were a born male chauvinist!"

"Only when it comes to my wife," he elaborated, turning in the car seat and resting one arm along the back. Phoebe found herself very aware of the silence, the warmth of the car, and the power of his presence. She clutched Ferd's cage tightly and waited.

"What is it exactly that you want from a wife?" she heard herself say very softly, almost breathlessly.

"I want a Phoebe Hampton who is so in love with me she won't worry about who I am or what I am. She'll be willing to have my children and, if necessary, she'll compromise all her fine thoughts on a career. She won't care if I have designs on her relationship to a brilliant and wealthy brother. She'll create a home for me, entertain my business friends as necessary but be happy to escape to the mountains or the sea, and clean the fish I catch. She'll have eyes only for me and never look at another tall, dark, and handsome man again in her life, having discovered that she much prefers a redhaired, blue-eyed man who will never have cause to suspect her loyalty . . ."

Phoebe stared at him, uncertain how to take the intensity of his tone and the grimness of his expression. For a moment she wavered on her own emotions and then the ever-present sense of humor came to her rescue. She deliberately controlled a giggle and fixed him with a gentle, understanding, worshipful look.

"You want a woman who would follow you barefoot wherever you chose to lead?" she suggested in dulcet tones, almost batting her long lashes at him, but managing to restrain herself.

"Exactly," he agreed, obviously pleased at her comprehension.

"That's funny," she went on cordially. "I would very much like to find a man who would do all those things for me! No wonder men like the idea of having a wife!"

Harlan lunged for her, but Phoebe was already

grabbing at the door handle and twisting herself and the bird cage out of the car. The laughter rippled in her throat as she stepped quickly out of reach and stood looking down at him.

Harlan, having missed in his first attempt, moved more slowly across the leather seat and climbed out to stand beside her with a mockingly dangerous expression.

"You," he stated, "are sadly in need of a husband! Not many men, if they knew what they were getting into, would be willing to assume the responsibility! I'm certain the Third never realized how incorrigible you are or he would have dropped the notion of marrying you after the first date! You're lucky to have found someone like me, Phoebe Hampton, who will take charge of such a trying specimen of the modern, liberated woman and teach her a basic fact of life!"

"Which is?" Phoebe demanded lightly, meeting the glitter of his eyes in the moonlight.

He stretched out a firm hand and rested it heavily on her shoulder, guiding her toward the house.

"Why, that she won't be truly happy until she's given herself, body and soul, to the right man!"

"My, you do have a fine opinion of yourself, don't you?" Phoebe grinned admiringly.

"Let's just say I know what I want and I won't be satisfied until I get it." He halted in front of the door, hunting for the key. A moment later he twisted the knob and greeted Jinx who came bounding forth to meet them with a cheerful yelp.

"Easy, boy. Remember your friend, Phoebe?"

Phoebe stretched down a hand to pat the dog. At that moment Ferd, sensing a new presence on the other side of his cage cover, chirped warningly.

Jinx froze.

Phoebe lifted the cage a bit higher, just in case the

128

hunting dog instincts in Jinx couldn't tell the difference between a parakeet and a pheasant.

"Jinx, this is a friend of mine," she began cautiously. "Love me, love my bird . . ."

"Behave yourself, Jinx," Harlan began firmly. "Ferd wouldn't even make a mouthful!"

"Harlan, darling! What's going on here?" A new voice from the darkened living room made Phoebe glance away from the tableau of dog and bird. It was her turn to freeze.

"Cynthia!" Harlan sounded genuinely startled, Phoebe decided. "What the hell are you doing here?"

"Poor Harlan," Phoebe muttered at his side, watching the golden vision glide toward them in the moonlight which illuminated the room through an endless wall of windows. "You must spend half your life asking women what the hell they're doing creeping up on you!"

He swiveled an angry glance down at her and then refocused his attention on the blond as she came to a halt in front of him and turned a green-eyed gaze up to him.

Phoebe felt herself turning very cold and came to the conclusion that spending the night in her own apartment would have been much more enjoyable, regardless of the questions raised by the open window. Why were there so many beautiful blonds in the world? Thin ones, at that! She absorbed the graceful picture the unknown Cynthia made dressed in a flowing garment of some slinky white material which draped beautifully over a perfectly carved, delicate figure.

"Waiting for you, naturally. I let myself in with the key you leave hidden outside. Remember showing me the spot? Jinx knows me and he certainly doesn't mind, do you, boy?" Cynthia turned an amused glance toward the dog but Jinx was still poised, transfixed, in front of an equally transfixed Phoebe. Only Ferd seemed able to react and he was beginning to sound agitated over the change in his routine.

"I smell the blood of an Oregonian!" he chirped with great ferocity in his tiny voice. Jinx quivered.

"Who's this, darling? Aren't you going to introduce me?" Cynthia stepped closer to Harlan and rested a delicate hand on his sleeve. The action seemed to bring him out of the trance he'd been in for the past several seconds.

"Cynthia, this is Phoebe Hampton. Phoebe, this is Cynthia Prescott. All right, the introductions are over. Kindly explain what you're doing inside my home, Cynthia." Harlan began to take charge again, reaching out to snap on a light switch, and flicking a warning look at Phoebe who had begun edging toward the door, bird cage held high. Jinx moved forward a fraction of an inch to follow.

"Stand still, Phoebe," Harlan growled. "You're not going anywhere. Cynthia?" he prompted firmly, confronting her as she stood looking helpless and beautiful, green eyes wide with innocent surprise.

"Harlan? What's wrong? You know I often spend the night here! I got back into town earlier than I expected so I thought I'd come on over and say hello."

"Did you? Well, as you can see, I'm otherwise occupied this evening so I suggest you take yourself off," Harlan replied coolly, not bothering to confirm or deny Cynthia's statement that she frequently spent the night. Phoebe decided glumly that meant it was probably true.

"But, darling!" Cynthia began in a throaty, pleading voice. "I've been longing to see you. You're the reason I came back early from Hawaii. I've thought over the things we said to each other before I left and I realize I made a mistake . . ."

130

"Cynthia, I'm not going to stand here discussing the matter with you tonight! It's late and I've got other plans. Please leave before I lose my temper completely and throw you out!"

Harlan's voice sounded altogether harsher and more determined than it had when he had confronted her in the cabin clearing and told her to leave, Phoebe thought wonderingly. If what Cynthia was implying was true, then she, Phoebe, had come into Harlan's life just after he'd been through a lover's quarrel. Perhaps he'd been put off beautiful blonds temporarily and that was the reason Phoebe had appealed for a time? She clutched her bird cage and stared at the other woman, wondering how to salvage her own pride. The thought was immediately followed by the depressing idea that her pride might not be the most important part of her needing to be saved. Her heart was unexpectedly in much greater danger.

"Oh, darling, are you still upset with me? You know how quickly I lose my temper and say things I don't really mean! I don't blame you for trying to teach me a lesson by seeing someone else but now that I'm back, ready to apologize, you can . . ." Her words jerked to a halt as Harlan grabbed hold of the slender hand which had been touching his arm and hauled Cynthia ruthlessly toward the door.

"Out!"

The green eyes filled with lovely, unshed tears, making the woman look like a drowned flower, Phoebe thought unhappily, remembering how her own face turned blotchy and red when she cried.

Harlan had Cynthia through the door and Phoebe heard him demanding to know where the woman had parked her car. There was a soft response which Phoebe couldn't catch and then the couple disappeared down the drive. Phoebe continued staring after them until a tiny movement by Jinx broke her paralysis.

"Traitor!" she hissed at the dog who favored her with a brief glance before returning his attention to the covered cage. "How could you let another woman in here? What kind of a watch dog are you, anyway?" Phoebe stepped back. "No, you can't have Ferd. He's about the only friend I have left in this world!"

Phoebe glanced out the open door toward the Jaguar, wondering if Harlan had taken the keys out of the ignition. Probably. She wasn't altogether sure she could drive it successfully enough to back it down the drive anyway. She turned to set Ferd's cage down on a nearby table and went to sit primly in a large overstuffed chair. She let her gaze wander around the room, taking in the plush green carpet, the modern, comfortable furniture and the incredible view of the city through the expanse of windows. There was a deck leading off the living room, a number of interesting, framed wall hangings which appeared to be Asian in design, and a sophisticated stereo system. A pleasant, subtly-done room, Phoebe decided, and automatically wondered if the beautiful Cynthia had helped in the design.

What did Harlan want with a woman like that, anyway? Of course, she *was* beautiful but couldn't he see the cold, calculating look in those green eyes? Probably not. Men were notoriously short-sighted when it came to lovely creatures like that. Phoebe wondered what they had quarreled over which had sent Cynthia off in a huff to Hawaii. Marriage? How long had the woman been Harlan's mistress? Phoebe jumped as the front door closed and Harlan strode loudly into the room.

Phoebe looked up at him as he came to a halt in front of her, hands on his hips. The hard set of his mouth and eyes did not invite questions, she thought.

"On the subject of Cynthia, I will make only one

132

comment and that is that she and I are through. You're not to concern yourself with her, Phoebe. Is that understood?'' Harlan regarded her forcefully, blue eyes hooded.

''You have lipstick on your cheek, Harlan,'' she said gently.

''Damn it to hell! Women!'' Harlan turned on his well-shod heel and disappeared down a hall, presumably in search of a bathroom mirror.

Phoebe was still sitting in the overstuffed chair when he returned, a small overnight bag in one hand, the lipstick gone.

''Shall we be going? Come on, Jinx!'' Harlan snapped his fingers but whether it was to secure the obedience of herself or the dog, Phoebe wasn't certain. Without a word she removed Ferd's cage from the table and followed Jinx out the door behind Harlan. Harlan stuffed everyone into the Jag and then climbed into the driver's seat with an economy of motion which amply demonstrated his current mood. With a muted roar, the car was backed efficiently down the drive and back onto the curving road.

Phoebe said nothing as they climbed a couple more miles into the hills and Harlan made no effort to start a conversation, either. He brought the vehicle to a halt in another drive, this one surrounded by a massive lawn and perfectly trimmed hedges. He slammed out of the car. Before Phoebe could struggle out of her side of the car with Ferd, he had her door opened and was reaching in to take the cage.

Phoebe stood gazing up at the beautiful old Victorian home in front of her with admiration. It was totally different in style from Harlan's house and carried the elegant patina of age.

''My grandfather had it built,'' Harlan broke the self-imposed silence to inform her, indicating the old house with a nod.

"The family mansion?" Phoebe asked calmly. "The one where two generations of Garands have been born and raised?" She could be cool, too, damn it!

"Yes, but not where the next will be raised!"

"Cynthia doesn't like this place?" Phoebe could have bitten her tongue out for the catty words, but it was too late.

"I don't like the place!" he snapped, handing her the bird cage. He led the way toward the imposing front door and set a heavy finger on the door bell. Almost immediately a light went on in an upstairs window. A few seconds later it was thrust open and a handsome woman in her sixties stared down at them.

"Harlan Garand! You look like you're leading a parade! What's going on?" a firm voice demanded.

Phoebe felt her humor momentarily come alive again at the thought of the picture they made standing on Aunt Flo's doorstep. Harlan, followed by a woman in an evening gown holding a cage, followed by a large, black dog.

"I'm bringing my future wife home to meet the family! What else would I be doing here at this hour of the night, Flo?" Harlan grinned up at the woman. "Aren't you going to let us in?"

"I'd do better to switch on a tape recorder and have you repeat those words!" The window slammed shut and a light was turned on inside the hall a short time later. In another moment the door was flung wide and a tall, striking woman, her grey hair in wild disarray, stood there examining Harlan and his entourage with eager, blue eyes—the same blue as Harlan's, Phoebe thought.

"So this is Phoebe? Come in, come in, my dear! You can't have any idea how anxious I've been to meet you! Ever since Harlan called this morning to tell me about his weekend I've been beside myself with impatience! I must admit, however, that you chose a strange time to bring her around, Harlan!''

"There's been another small adventure, Flo," Harlan told her, pushing Phoebe ahead of him, into the hall. "When I brought Phoebe home tonight, her bedroom window was open. She's fairly sure she left it closed and since that other kidnapper is still loose, I thought it would be a good idea to have her spend the next few days elsewhere!''

"The next few days!" Phoebe gasped. "I thought you meant I'd only spend the night here!" She turned at once to her hostess. "Please, Miss Garand, I have no intention of imposing on you for any longer than this evening! I had no idea Harlan meant me to stay for a few days!''

"Call me Flo, Phoebe, and of course you'll stay! Just as long as Harlan thinks it's necessary! I see we're going to have Jinx to protect us, too. That was nice of you, Harlan . . .''

"You're going to have Jinx and me too!" he corrected, leaning forward to give his aunt a kiss on the cheek. "I considered taking Phoebe to my house but she's talked me into this crazy idea of a courtship and she's afraid that once I have her safely tucked into my bed the yellow roses and candlelight dinners will cease!''

"Harlan!" Phoebe protested furiously. "How dare you talk like that! Don't you have any conscience at all? Doesn't it bother you in the least to embarrass me in front of your aunt?" The nerve of the man!

"Don't worry about it, Phoebe!" Florence Garand chuckled delightedly. "I've known him a lot longer than you have and tried for a number of years to control him. I assure you, it's hopeless! Do tell me all about this evening, Phoebe. You're certain you left your window shut?" As she spoke Harlan's aunt was leading the way up a carved staircase, its treads covered in a rich plum

135

colored rug.

"Well, as certain as I can be. Of course, there's always the possibility I simply forgot and left it open. Normally I wouldn't have thought twice about it, but the weekend made me a tad nervous!" Phoebe confided, following the woman with Ferd's cage. Harlan brought up the rear, carrying the overnight bags.

"A tad! Good grief, my dear! From what Harlan told me, you went through enough to drive a sensible person to a nervous breakdown!"

"Well, perhaps a fit of the vapors," Phoebe temporized, thinking that the house was made for fainting heroines, perhaps not slightly plump, sensible heroines in glasses, though.

"I think you were amazingly brave about the whole thing! Plus, you managed to free yourself too! And then having to contend with Harlan on top of everything else!" Flo hesitated beside a door in the upstairs hall and pushed it open. "Will this do for tonight? It's already made up. If you find another bedroom you prefer tomorrow we can always have it prepared."

"This is lovely, Flo," Phoebe smiled appreciatively as she glanced around at the huge four-poster bed, flowered wall paper and fluffy white rug. "I shall feel like a Victorian lady tonight!" She walked into the room happily.

"She looks a bit like a lady from the last century, doesn't she, Aunt Flo?" Harlan interrupted, lounging in the doorway behind them. "I mean she's not skinny and hard looking like most modern women!"

"Harlan, I'm not in a mood to be teased about my figure tonight!" Phoebe warned, whirling to confront his lazy grin. She wouldn't mention Cynthia in front of his aunt and he probably knew it, but that didn't mean she had forgotten! She turned her back on him and set down Ferd's cage.

"Harlan, she's right! Stop teasing her. It's late and the poor girl's been through enough. You know where your room is. Why don't you take yourself and your dog off and go to bed? I'll take care of Phoebe!" Flo ordered.

"Yes, ma'am. Goodnight, Flo. Goodnight, Phoebe." Harlan stepped forward, dropping a dutiful kiss on the cheek of each woman and did as ordered. Jinx, with a last wistful glance at the bird cage, followed.

"I admire the way you handle him," Phoebe said fervently, sinking down onto the thick bed.

"It comes with experience. Don't worry, you'll soon get the hang of it." Florence smiled kindly, a definite twinkle in the bright blue eyes. "Yes, you look as if you'll do very well for Harlan. He needs a real woman. To think of all the time I've wasted trying to find one for him and then he ups and discovers his own! So much for matchmaking!" Flo turned back toward the door.

"There's a connecting bath through that door and my room's at the end of the hall if you need anything. There will be a woman arriving at six o'clock to fix breakfast and take care of some of the chores. Harlan said you work so I imagine you'll want to eat early? Six-thirty all right?"

"Yes, thank you," Phoebe smiled gratefully. "You've been very kind, Flo."

"Nonsense! I'm delighted to have you here! I'll catch up on the details tomorrow but for now you'd better get some sleep!" She was gone in a swirl of pink housecoat.

Phoebe looked over at Ferd's cage and after a bit got up to go across and remove the cover.

"Well, Ferd, what do you think?" she asked softly, opening the door to his cage and inserting her finger. Ferd stepped aboard, eyeing her thoughtfully as he rode the finger outside.

"Fee, fie, fo, fum," he finally announced as if it were the last word on the subject.

"Succinct and to the point," Phoebe commented. "But I was hoping for sympathy, not common sense. Back you go! It's time you were asleep, anyway!"

Breakfast the next morning was an informal affair served in a sunny old-fashioned nook the Victorian architect had specifically designed for the first meal of the day. When Phoebe descended the stairs promptly at six-thirty, dressed in the neat suit she had packed the night before, it was to find her hostess already seated and reading the morning paper.

"Phoebe! Good morning! How did you sleep?"

"Perfectly, Flo. How about you? I hope our midnight arrival didn't upset your rest too much?" Phoebe took a chair and reached enthusiastically for the silver coffee pot. There was real cream, too!

"Best night's sleep I've had since Harlan announced he was going to build his own home!" Flo grinned.

Phoebe looked at her sharply, wondering where Harlan was. He was supposed to drive her to work this morning . . .

"Why did you sleep well that time?" she asked. "Had he been getting underfoot around the house?"

"Oh, no. I was happy to have him with me after he returned. He'd been living in the Far East, managing one of the offices Garand has there. When my brother died, he did his duty and returned to Portland. But I knew he didn't want to leave Hong Kong and he didn't exactly welcome the idea of the increased responsibility of running the whole operation. That was two years ago. It took him a year to adjust and decide to keep the business. For a time, I was sure he might well the whole thing to an outsider! When he came home one day and said he planned to build on a nice lot a couple of miles from here, I realized he was staying."

"I gather the feeling of family tradition has caught up with him," Phoebe agreed drily. "He's even talking about an heir!"

"I'm so glad! He's shown no interest whatsoever in the women he's met during the past two years. Heaven knows, I did my best to find a suitable wife for him but he got furious every time! I guess he's one of those men who has to come to terms with things in his own style. I have the impression he did a much better job of selecting a companion that I was doing."

"Thank you, but it isn't exactly settled yet, Flo. I mean, you know how Harlan is, always plowing into things, determined to have it all his way. We've only known each other since Saturday morning and I'm not at all sure . . ."

"Not at all sure you want to wait until after the Rose Festival to get married? Why didn't you say so, sweetheart? I'll be happy to advance the date! How about this Friday?" Harlan swooped through the door, a bunch of yellow roses in one hand, and Jinx romping at his heels. His hair was still damp from the shower, red tendrils curling at the back, and he appeared amazingly fresh. He planted a husbandly kiss on her startled lips.

"Harlan, you know perfectly well I didn't mean that! I was explaining to your aunt how we hardly know each other . . ." Phoebe's words were cut off as the wet roses were thrust into her surprised grasp.

"Mind the thorns, honey. Have you got a vase for these, Flo?"

"I've got rose vases stored all over this house. You know that! Just a second and I'll dig one out!" Florence disappeared in the direction of the kitchen.

"Harlan! I do wish you wouldn't give your aunt the definite idea that we're going to be married! She'll be so disappointed if it doesn't work out!" Phoebe scolded, frowning at him as he took a seat across from her. He thrust a coffee cup in her direction and she found herself automatically pouring his morning coffee like any good wife. Irritated, she set the silver pot down heavily and glared at him.

"Don't look at me like that, honey! A wife is supposed to be sweet and loving and full of cheer at this hour of the morning! Besides, what are you mad about? You got your roses, didn't you? Fresh from Flo's garden. You'll have to see it, Phoebe! It's magnificent. Growing roses is a major hobby here in Portland, you know! People here take it quite seriously . . ."

"I'm aware of Portland's interest in roses, Harlan. We're discussing something else entirely . . ." Phoebe was forced to cease her lecture as Harlan's aunt appeared, carrying a magnificent crystal vase filled with water.

"Thank you, Flo," she smiled, carefully setting the gorgeous roses into the crystal. "Ummm. They're beautiful!" Phoebe took a moment to inhale the fragrance, the curve of her hair swinging toward as she leaned over them.

"Eat your breakfast, Phoebe. I want to get to work early. Don't forget I'm picking you up at noon so we can select a ring!" Harlan ordered, pouring cream over his cereal and helping himself to the toast. He smiled at his aunt.

"I haven't had a chance to tell you, but Phoebe is a terrific cook. In fact, that was how she convinced me to let her stay on Saturday morning. I was all set to hustle her back down the mountain but before I knew what was happening she was feeding me!"

Flo laughed. "The surest way to a man's heart. There's always a grain of truth in those old sayings! I expect it's instinct for a man to look with favor on a woman who can cook! Just as it's instinct for a woman to be drawn toward a strong, dominant man!"

Phoebe gagged on a bit of cereal and choked embarrassingly until Harlan's hand landed with a thud in the middle of her back. Then she managed to regain her composure.

"Phoebe isn't accustomed to the idea of having a man around to keep her in line," he explained kindly to his aunt. "She's been used to giving the orders and she's got a little adjusting to do!"

"Give me one good reason why a woman should be attracted to a domineering male except in a romantic novel!" Phoebe demanded grimly, casting a decided glare at Harlan.

"You read those too? I'm so glad. We'll have to go through our collections and compare!" Flo enthused. "But the reason why women love such men is quite obvious, isn't it? A man who shows he can take care of himself and exerts some control over his environment is a man who can care for and protect a woman and her children too. It's a survival characteristic, if you ask me!"

"You see, Phoebe? No need to fight an instinct," Harlan chimed in teasingly.

"There is never an excuse for bullying someone else!" Phoebe fought back, feeling outnumbered but determined not to surrender easily.

"Does Harlan bully you?" Flo asked with great curiosity, staring at her nephew as if she hadn't seen him before.

"Horribly! I'll have you know he even made me clean his fish after he caught them!"

"Simple division of labor principle!" Harlan defended himself. "Anyway, she deserved it for crashing my weekend!"

Flo's laughter halted the battle and she sobered only after a great effort. "You two are great together! That settles it! Seeing you face each other over the breakfast table has removed any doubt I might have had. We'll have the engagement party this Saturday night!"

141

chapter eight

"Harlan, what are we going to do? We've got to stop your aunt before she goes ahead and plans an engagement party!" Phoebe groaned as the Jag was brought to a halt in front of her company's towering downtown office building. She had been remonstrating futilely with the man at the wheel ever since they had left the house and had gotten precisely nowhere.

"Why? We're going to be married so I don't see why we shouldn't have the party." Harlan switched off the ignition and leaned over to pull her against him. "Stop worrying! It will be a small affair—especially with such little notice. Aunt Flo won't overwhelm you with strangers, if that's what's concerning you, honey." He paused. "That reminds me, we must phone your brother."

"You know damn well what's concerning me!"

"Now don't go getting upset with small things . . ."

"Small things! You think Cynthia Prescott is a *small* thing?" Phoebe felt her voice rise into a higher register and was helpless to keep it from happening. Visions of the golden Cynthia had haunted her dreams during the night and the other woman's beauty was as fresh in Phoebe's mind this morning as it had been last night in the moonlight.

"I told you to forget Cynthia!"

"I'm finding that rather difficult! My God, Harlan!

It was obvious she felt quite at home in your house last night!'' Phoebe blazed.

"So? I make no apologies for my past. It should be meaningless to you just as yours is meaningless to me. It's the present and the future we're concerned with and don't you forget it!'' With that, Harlan yanked her tightly against his chest and crushed her furious lips beneath his mouth, holding her with both hands in a grip that Phoebe knew was going to leave bruises.

Phoebe struggled desperately for a long, painful moment and then gave up in despair. How could she fight him when he held her so closely? His kiss, his arms—when she was experiencing them—were the only things that mattered in the whole world. It was depressing to be so much in the power of a man, she told herself. It was also exciting and exhilarating beyond words. She felt herself relax as Harlan's mouth took hers fiercely.

"Damn!'' he muttered thickly against her lips, "But I wish we were anywhere else but here on a city street at seven-thirty in the morning! I'd show you how pointless it is to fight me, Phoebe, honey. You want me as much as I want you! Why don't you do us both a favor and admit it?'' His hands moved, shaping her waist beneath the jacket of her suit and then sliding along the softness of her blouse to the fullness of her breast.

"Harlan!'' she managed to beg. "Someone will see us!''

"So?''

"This is Portland! Things aren't done that way here!''

He sighed. "All right. But don't think you can keep putting me off. I can tell you right now you're going to wind up in my bed before the next three weeks are over!'' He set her away from him with an air of determination. "I'll be back at noon. See that you're waiting here on the front steps!"

Phoebe removed herself from the car, feeling weak and shaky. She didn't trust herself to speak so she slammed the Jag's heavy door and turned to march up the steps of the office building. It was only as she glanced back over her shoulder to make sure Harlan had driven off that she saw Richard standing on the sidewalk below, staring at her. It was too much. She couldn't face another male just then. Phoebe fled through the revolving doors and into the elevator.

An hour later Phoebe glanced up from a monthly report she was writing to answer the phone.

"Phoebe Hampton? This is Cynthia Prescott. We met last night." The saccharin sweet tones made Phoebe's skin crawl. What a morning this was developing into, she thought dismally.

"Yes, Miss Prescott? What can I do for you?" she said in her most businesslike voice, trying to imply she was being rudely interrupted.

"I thought you deserved an explanation for that small scene last night. I mean, I know I'd very much want to know what was going on in a similar situation!" A throaty little chuckle followed. The woman to woman approach, thought Phoebe grimly.

"Harlan explained what little needed explaining, thank you," she said firmly.

"Oh, no need to be coy about it, Phoebe. We both know a man couldn't begin to give an adequate explanation of that sort of thing—especially as infuriated a man as Harlan was last night. He's really something in a temper, isn't he? But perhaps you haven't known him long enough to learn his various moods?"

"What is it you want, Miss Prescott?" Phoebe pressed coldly.

144

"Just to give you a word of warning, my dear. I've been acquainted with Harlan for a lot longer than you have and we've been through a good deal together, including a number of lovers' quarrels. I admit this last one was my fault, what with refusing to marry him as soon as he wished, but he'll come around. He always does. It might be hard on you, though, if he used you to take revenge against me. That's why I'm calling. Don't let him talk you into doing anything drastic while he's upset with me. As soon as he recovers his temper he'll want me back and it would be a shame if you got hurt in the process!"

Phoebe couldn't believe it! She had heard of women who threatened other women over a man but she'd never been in such a position before in her life! Desperately she tried to think how to deal with this awful person on the other end of the line. At that moment several years of business experience came to her aid. One fought fire with fire.

"It's very thoughtful of you to warn me, Miss Prescott," Phoebe began coolly. "But I happen to know Harlan is a man who takes what he wants. If he'd wanted you badly enough as his wife, you would have been married to him by now. Please don't concern yourself over my welfare. I can handle him and you both. Don't forget, I'm the one who stayed behind last night. The woman in possession, Miss Prescott, is the woman with the advantage. Don't bother calling again!" Phoebe hung up the phone carefully. Where had Cynthia gotten her number, she wondered.

She was still mulling that one over when twelve o'clock arrived and she reluctantly headed toward the elevator. Harlan wouldn't appreciate being kept waiting. Visions of him storming into the building in quest of her, made Phoebe move more quickly.

The Jag was double-parked directly in front of the building. It was typical of Harlan to pull a stunt like that in the height of midday traffic!

"I was just about to come and find you," he announced, leaning across the seat to open the door.

"That thought had occurred to me!" she responded feelingly, slipping into the soft leather.

"Good. You're learning," he grinned and pulled into traffic with casual disregard for other drivers. Or at least it appeared casual but Phoebe was willing to bet he knew exactly what he was doing!

"Harlan, don't you think we should wait a while for the ring?" Phoebe tried one last time. "We've still got three weeks to go and so much could happen in that length of time!" Such as my meeting a few more Cynthias, she added to herself.

"I told you, honey, I want my ring on your finger. I'm not prepared to risk losing a good cook like you!" He seemed absolutely determined to be cheerful and enthusiastic, Phoebe thought resentfully.

A few minutes later he had parked the Jag in a downtown garage and was hurrying her along the sidewalk toward a prosperous looking jewelry store.

"Come in, Mr. Garand! We've been expecting you!" a sturdy gentleman in a refined suit greeted them as soon as they were inside the door. "Right this way. I've done my best to prepare a fine selection for your perusal. I do hope you'll find something you like!" Beaming his confidence in his wares, the man led them toward a private table and indicated they should be seated in the plush chairs. Wordlessly, Phoebe watched as several velvet lined trays were spread before her.

"Harlan," she finally whispered frantically, feeling the walls closing in quickly. "Let's talk about this some more . . ."

"Choose, Phoebe, my dear, or I'll do it for you!"

She looked up into his face and saw there what she had seen the day he had forced her to clean the fish. She had learned her lesson that day. In this mood, there was nothing for it but to comply.

"All right, Harlan," she agreed forlornly, gazing down at the glittering array before her.

Rings were held out for her approval and she dutifully tried them on, nodding her appreciation in an effort not to offend the jeweler. He had every right to be proud of the rings he was displaying. It wasn't his fault she was having trouble working up genuine interest.

Time passed and she began to get nervous. Harlan was determined that she make a selection before leaving. Finally, in desperation, she picked up a small gold ring set with an emerald. It didn't seem as flashy as its neighbors and Phoebe decided it was somewhat like her in that respect.

"Perfect. It matches your eyes when you're upset and yelling at me!" Harlan grinned. He took it from her limp hand and gave it into the jeweler's keeping. "You'll have it sized for us? We're having an engagement party on Saturday night and it would be great to have it by then . . ."

"Of course. You can pick it up tomorrow in fact, Mr. Garand," the jeweler nodded, smiling happily.

"That will be great. Come on, Phoebe. There's still time for a short lunch if we hurry. I'll take care of the purchase when I pick it up tomorrow, all right, Mr. Bernard?"

"That will be fine."

That afternoon at five o'clock, Harlan was again waiting for her in front of her building. Phoebe descended the steps reluctantly and got into the Jag with an air of resignation.

"Stop sulking, honey. I've told Aunt Flo we won't be home for dinner. I'll drive by your apartment so you can change and we'll go out to eat."

"More candlelight and wine?"

"The best I can find. There's one other item on the agenda. We're going to call your brother. He'll want to be at his sister's engagement party."

Her brother's startled exclamation over the phone line half an hour later was sufficiently loud to reach Harlan who was standing several feet away.

"I know it's rather sudden, Steve, but I promise to tell you the whole story when you get here . . ." Phoebe began cautiously.

"Is he there?" Steve Hampton demanded.

"Well, yes, as a matter of fact, he is. We're going out to dinner . . ."

"Put him on the line!"

Without a word Phoebe handed the phone to Harlan who accepted it willingly enough.

"How do you do, Steve?" he began cheerfully. "Before you get upset about the fact that I'm marrying your sister, let me answer a few of your questions before you have a chance to ask. One, I am quite able to financially support Phoebe. Two, the family line is very good. Garands have been in Portland for a century. That's a long time on the West Coast, you know. And three, I can handle Phoebe! What?" Harlan listened for a moment and then a slow smile began to shape the line of his mouth. "Yes, I agree with you. Number three is the most important item on the list! If you recognize that, I think we'll discover that we think alike on important issues!" Harlan perched himself on the phone table and threw Phoebe a look which said clearly that what was coming next was strictly man-to-man talk. With a disgusted word, she turned and walked out of the room, leaving the two most important men in her life alone to get to know each other over the telephone.

The pattern for the rest of the week was established. Harlan drove Phoebe to work every morning and fetched her at night. He greeted her with yellow roses over the breakfast table daily and kept her out late at night dancing. By Friday morning Phoebe was a nervous wreck. Her brother was due to arrive Saturday morning and she had yet to make hotel reservations for him as he had stated firmly he did not wish to stay at Flo's. She hadn't argued with him, although it would have been nice to have him close. She knew he always preferred to stay in a hotel when he visited. He had an ingrained fear of imposing on people, he claimed, but Phoebe privately thought her brother simply liked having the freedom of a hotel atmosphere. He was a man who liked his own company. And in his line of work, privacy was a valuable commodity. It gave him the opportunity for creative thinking which was so important.

"Too many late nights for this girl, Harlan," Flo opined across the breakfast table Friday morning. "You're wearing her out!" She eyed Phoebe assessingly.

"I'm wearing her down!" Harlan corrected unrepentantly. "Here, Phoebe, have some more coffee. You do look a little slow moving this morning!"

"Thank you and may I say you're looking quite well yourself?" she muttered.

"Stop teasing her, Harlan," Flo said seriously. "If you don't want it to appear as if you've taken to beating her, I suggest you bring her home early tonight and let the poor thing get some sleep!"

"Oh, all right. But it will probably be a mistake. Haven't you noticed how much more obedient she's been when she's tired?" Harlan inquired of his aunt as he spread jam on his toast.

"What are you going to wear tomorrow night, Phoebe?" Florence demanded in a determined effort to change the subject.

"Frankly, I haven't given it a moment's thought!" Phoebe responded crushingly.

"Well, don't you worry about it. Tomorrow morning we'll get rid of His Highness here and go shopping. Pam has everything well in hand for the party, as usual and there'll be no need for us to do anything but appear tomorrow night!"

True to her word, Flo took Phoebe shopping Saturday morning to several very small, very elegant boutiques she had not yet discovered herself. When she got a look at the price tags, Phoebe decided it was just as well she hadn't. But at last a gently draped gown in colors of the sea was located, much to Flo's satisfaction.

"The color of your eyes, my dear. It's gorgeous!"

Steve Hampton arrived shortly before noon and Harlan took Phoebe to the airport to meet him. She had a moment's worry as the tall man with the dark brown hair and the almost-green eyes so much like her own walked toward them from the ramp. She took an uncertain step forward, meeting her brother's demanding gaze unflinchingly. Then she was hugging him affectionately as he smiled over the top of her head at the redhaired man behind her.

"I only hope," Steve told Harlan, shaking hands cordially, "that you know what you're getting yourself into!"

"At least I won't ever be bored!" Harlan grinned.

"Well, little sister, so you did your own matchmaking

150

this time!" Steve smiled down at Phoebe as the three of them moved toward the luggage claim area. "I have to admit I couldn't have fixed you up better myself! This one doesn't even need to have the family finances straightened out!"

"Steve!" Phoebe gasped, mortified. And then, seeing that Harlan didn't appear to be offended she demanded, "How did you know? You only have Harlan's word that he can support me!"

"Don't be ridiculous, Phoebe," Harlan chuckled. "Your brother has spent the time since our phone call having me thoroughly checked out, haven't you, Steve?"

"Of course," Steve agreed readily. "Wouldn't you have done the same?"

Harlan nodded. "Naturally."

Phoebe looked from one to the other suspiciously. "Are you two serious? You would sic private detectives on each other before you would let him marry into the family?" Their answering nods of confirmation told her all she needed to know.

"Men!" she groaned, not for the first time.

Phoebe descended the carved staircase at eight o'clock, as ordered by Flo, to find Harlan waiting for her at the bottom. She paused a few steps from the last stair, filling herself with the sight of the lean, utterly masculine length of him. The evening jacket fitted him to perfection and the whiteness of it contrasted with the rich red of his hair gleaming in the light of the hall chandelier. Dark slacks and shoes polished to an elegant gloss combined with the silk of his shirt to lend him an understated tone of quiet elegance. He looked, Phoebe thought abruptly, tall, redhaired, and handsome—every woman's dream.

Harlan watched her come slowly down the last few

steps without saying a word, brilliant eyes going over her from head to foot in an almost hungry glance.

"You are perfect," he said in a low, husky voice, reaching out to take her hand. "And you're mine."

Phoebe stared at him wordlessly, trying desperately to read the depth of his feelings in the hard planes of his face.

"Oh, Harlan. Are you sure? Really sure?"

He smiled. "Positive." And then he put a hand into a jacket pocket and removed a small case. A jeweler's case.

"My ring," Phoebe murmured, fascinated as he opened the small object and removed the delicate emerald. He slid it easily onto her finger and then raised her hand lightly to his lips. There was an attitude of finality about the procedure as if the act of placing his ring on her finger sealed them together. Phoebe trembled with the overpowering sensation of being told in no uncertain manner that she was his. Her eyes met his and he leaned forward to touch her lips lightly with his own.

"My own, cuddly Phoebe!" he smiled wickedly into her wide eyes.

"And I can cook, too," she breathed, groping for a response which wouldn't sound as if she had lost her composure completely.

"What more could a man ask?"

"All right, you two, time to stop admiring each other and prepare to greet your guests. I hear a car now," Flo instructed, coming into the hall from the living room. She was followed by a smiling Steve whose expression widened into a grin as he caught sight of his sister's face.

After that Phoebe lost track of time. She obediently greeted guests, relying on the experience she'd had with people to get her over difficult moments. She stood and chatted in small groups, answering questions easily, skipping lightly over the ones which threatened to pry too deeply into her association with Harlan. Either Flo or Harlan stayed by her side for the first hour, making sure she was comfortable with their friends and parrying the questions with her. When one was with her, the other was with her brother who quickly found himself in an interested circle of men demanding to know about patents and royalties and licensing.

Phoebe had just caught a glimpse of Steve's head in the crowd and was thinking of gravitating in his direction when she was stopped by a voice at her elbow.

"I understand you only recently met Harlan?" an elderly dowager queried pointedly.

"Harlan is the type of man who sweeps a woman off her feet," Phoebe smiled blandly, not bothering to elaborate on the exact time of the meeting or the location.

"Someone told me you ran into each other in the mountains over the weekend?" the woman persisted, her diamond earrings flashing heavily in the elegantly lit room.

"What else could I do but marry the girl after an incident like that?" Harlan chuckled, coming up behind Phoebe and planting a tiny kiss on her shoulder. The warmth in his eyes and the very proprietary little caress was not lost on his listeners who smiled in response.

Around ten o'clock Phoebe managed to escape to the refreshment table. Her appetite which had deserted her at dinner, returned in full force now that the first crucial hours of the party were behind her. She was studying the relative merits of shrimp canapés and small salmon sandwiches when a deep voice spoke behind her.

"Stick with the salmon sandwiches. The shrimp things are okay but not nearly as good."

"Thanks for the advice!" Phoebe chuckled, helping herself to a delicate sandwich and turning to face the voice. The movement of her head brought her eyes to the level of a handsome silk tie. She had to look at lot further to meet the steel grey eyes. Very tall, very dark, and very handsome, she thought calmly. The sight failed to move her at all. Nothing could now compete with red hair and blue eyes.

"I'm Phoebe Hampton," she smiled cheerfully.

"The guest of honor, of course. I arrived late and missed the introductions. I'm Matt Wentworth. Harlan and I know each other from business associations. How about some more of the champagne punch? I was just about to refill my own glass."

"That would be marvelous." Phoebe held out her glass obligingly and watched as he filled it carefully.

"Have you and Harlan set a date yet?" he inquired pleasantly.

"No. I mean, it's still a little up in the air. He's talking about some time after the Rose Festival . . ." Phoebe said politely. She couldn't very well say that Harlan had set more of a deadline than a date!

"That sounds like Harlan. Once he makes up his mind, not much can stand in his way! You looked very thoughtful as I came up behind you a moment ago. You must be glad to get a small break from the throng out there!" He motioned toward the noise of the party in the next room.

"Actually, I was just thinking tht I've been so busy this week I haven't even seen a newspaper! I was wondering how the market was doing. Very unromantic thoughts, I assure you!"

"You own some stock?" he pursued, sounding interested.

"I've been getting my feet wet for the past couple of years. Every so often I terrify myself and do something rash like buy an off-the-wall computer stock and then I get cold feet for a while, waiting to see what happens! I've been pretty lucky, though. My broker is excellent and I've done some studying on the subject."

"Keeping up with inflation, at least?"

"Better than that, on the whole." Phoebe smiled modestly.

"I knew it! I'm talking to a wizard! If you're doing better than keeping pace with inflation, I want to hear more!"

"Sorry, no tips! I have the feeling that as soon as I encourage someone to buy into the stocks I'm holding, the entire thing will collapse under me!"

"A healthy superstition. At least tell me the areas you're into?" he begged, beautifully white teeth revealed in an engaging smile.

"Well, energy companies have been doing well for me. Some electronics . . ."

"Tell me more. Would you mind if we moved out onto the terrace? It's getting warm in here." Without waiting for her agreement Matt Wentworth took her arm in a casual grip and guided her gently toward the open doors at the end of the room.

Phoebe, after a small hesitation, decided she was glad to have someone to talk to who wanted to discuss a subject other than her forthcoming marriage. She went with him willingly.

She was deep into a friendly argument about the future of the aerospace industry when a familiar, throaty laugh sounded from the other side of the hedge in the direction of Flo's rose garden. Cynthia Prescott.

Phoebe broke off her comment on a company engaged in building a new space shuttle to frown uncertainly.

"Something wrong, Phoebe?" Matt smiled curiously down at her.

"Nothing. Just thought I heard someone I know." She launched determinedly back into her subject, wondering when the other woman had arrived. But the laughter floated toward them again and this time when Phoebe glanced out toward the garden she saw a flash of movement. A woman in a long gown and a man in a white evening jacket. Harlan! She knew it was Harlan and he was with Cynthia. The wave of despair which swept over her in that moment was almost more than she could bear. He couldn't do this to her! Not at the engagement party he had insisted on holding!

"I think it's time we went back indoors, Matt," Phoebe said, the enthusiasm and interest drained from her voice.

The laughter trilled yet again and Matt glanced across the hedge. "I see Cynthia is up to her old tricks," he said softly. "Is her presence in the garden the reason for your sudden desire to go back to the party?"

"I don't think . . ."

"Come now. Going to give up so easily? I've known Miss Prescott for some time and I can guarantee you she won't respond to subtlety. If you want her out of your life, you're going to have to throw her out, I'm afraid!"

Don't get mad; get even. Phoebe lifted her head proudly. She caught Matt Wentworth's expectant, encouraging look and smiled shakily. The adrenalin began flowing through her, the way it did when she decided to challenge a superior at work. Matt was right. Some people didn't understand subtlety at all. Harlan might or might not be to blame but Cynthia Prescott would never be blameless.

"Perhaps a short walk through the garden before we return, Matt?" Phoebe felt her smile firm. That woman was no good for Harlan! Even if he had changed his mind about Phoebe, Cynthia was not the one he should think of using to replace her! Probably couldn't even cook! And she dreaded to think what kind of mother Cynthia would make!

"An excellent idea." Matt took her arm and they stepped off the terrace together, moving toward the path which led down through the rose garden and on to the stone goldfish pond—the path that would bring them face to face with Cynthia and Harlan.

The husky, sexy sound of Cynthia's voice became clearer now and Phoebe could hear Harlan's deeper tones occasionally. He wasn't laughing with her, Phoebe decided and wondered again which of the two was to blame for the jaunt into the rose garden. Matt guided her firmly around the last hedge and there on a bench sat Harlan and Cynthia. The other woman's floating gown seemed to have draped itself over the darkness of Harlan's slacks and her arm was in the act of moving up to his shoulder when she spotted Phoebe and Matt. She looked briefly startled and then the cat look came into the green eyes, visible in the moonlight, probably because, like a cat's, they shone in the dark, Phoebe thought grimly. She determined to get in the first word. Ignoring Harlan who was staring first at her and then at Matt with an expression of growing annoyance, Phoebe smiled her best business smile.

"Cynthia, darling! I've been looking all over for you, haven't I, Matt?" Phoebe moved forward quickly, leaning down to grasp the other woman's arm and help her to her feet. Cynthia resisted but she was smaller than Phoebe and, as Phoebe had often pointed out, some of the roundness was muscle. In a second she had Cynthia on her feet and was forcing her down the path toward the pond.

"Phoebe!" Harlan's voice came urgently behind her, "Where are you going?"

"Cynthia and I are going to have a little girl-to-girl chat. You know how it is. We have so much in common and so far we simply haven't found the time to discuss things thoroughly. I believe Matt wanted to speak to you, so this will be a perfect opportunity for all of us!" With a deadly sweet smile, Phoebe continued toward the pond, Cynthia's arm twisted in a painful grip.

"It's all right, Harlan," Matt said quietly behind them. "Phoebe won't come to any harm out here in the garden and I'm sure those two are dying to talk to each other. You know women!"

"I know Phoebe!" Harlan snapped. "She always gets her revenge . . ."

An instant later the voices of the men had faded so that the words could no longer be clearly distinguished. Phoebe pushed Cynthia through a row of bushes and brought her to a halt beside the pond.

"You want to talk to me, Phoebe Hampton? I'll talk! I'll tell you right now you don't stand a chance of holding Harlan! Who do you think you are, anyway? I've known him for years and he wants me! Can't you understand that? You may have had one flaming weekend up in the mountains but that was only because he was lonely and bored without me! He's a man and he's not above using a convenient woman! You may have put pressure on him through that crazy aunt of his but in the end he won't marry you, I promise! He's going to marry me!"

"Oh, shut up, Cynthia! Be honest with yourself! If Harlan had wanted you for a wife, you would have been married by now as I told you the other day on the phone. By the way, how did you find out where I worked? Just idle curiosity on my part, you realize. But it's been puzzling me."

"A friend told me." Cynthia glared at her.

"A friend?" Phoebe applied a bit more pressure to the arm she was holding.

"Julie Chambers, if you must know! Let go of my arm!"

"I didn't realize you knew Julie. I should have. You're two of a kind. Well, that's really the only matter I was curious about. The rest of our little discussion concerns Harlan. You will leave him alone, Miss Prescott, or I will personally see to it that you suffer some very severe consequences. The first of said consequences being a mild dip in the pond!" Before the lovely blond could grasp her intention, Phoebe stuck a foot around her ankle, pushed gently, and watched with great satisfaction as Cynthia fell backward into the pond, scattering lilly pads, splashing water and no doubt terrifying the fish. She only got out half a startled screech before she landed ignominiously on her backside.

"Phoebe!" Harlan hurried through the rose bushes, Matt following more sedately at his heels. "What the hell have you done with Cynthia?" He halted, frowning severely down at her and then turning to look at the furious blond struggling out of the pond. Phoebe could have sworn his lips twitched and he had to control a grin.

"Harlan, that woman is a menace! She threw me in here! I could have been badly hurt!" Cynthia's husky voice rose to a distinct screech as she looked down at the sopping gown. "Just look at me! Damn you, Phoebe Hampton . . ."

"What a pity, Miss Prescott. Too bad you slipped. But these stones here around the pond can be very

159

tricky. You'll have to rush right home and change before you catch your death of cold!''

"I'll be happy to see you to your car, Cynthia," Matt stepped around Harlan and took hold of the frustrated woman's arm. "You really are quite damp, aren't you? We'd better hurry!''

"But . . ." began Cynthia helplessly, turning for a last glare at Phoebe before being hustled off by Matt Wentworth.

"Quiet, Cynthia, or the entire party will hear you and come running to see what happened. It's going to be a little difficult to explain, isn't it?'' Matt counseled helpfuly as the two disappeared up the path toward the far side of the house. A long, tense silence settled over the garden as Phoebe was left alone with Harlan. She continued staring in the direction her rival had gone, the cool anger she had been experiencing beginning to disappear as quickly as it had come.

"Well, Phoebe Hampton, you're living up to your reputation, aren't you?'' Harlan's tones were unfathomable. Was he furious?

"That woman irritates me," Phoebe defended herself in a small voice.

"Apparently. Do you intend to spend the rest of our life throwing every woman who talks to me into a fish pond?'' Phoebe didn't dare look at him. She knew one red brow would be climbing warningly.

"Only the skinny blond ones," Phoebe managed with an effort at flippancy.

"I see. Just how did you happen to be in the garden with Matt, anyway?''

"I was . . . was talking to him on the terrace and we heard . . .''

"In other words you were having a private conversation with one of your favorite masculine types. I believe Matt would probably qualify as tall, dark, and

160

good looking?'' Harlan's voice had a distinctly unpleasant edge to it now.

"We were having an extremely casual conversation on the stock market, if you must know! He certainly wasn't draped all over me as Cynthia was with you!''

"Cynthia was in the process of saying goodbye!''

"The hell she was! I've been getting nothing but warnings from her all week on how she was going to get you back!'' Phoebe whirled, the soft skirts of her gown swirling around her ankles, and faced Harlan.

"I think we had better discuss the situation after the party, don't you?'' Harlan said coldly, stepping forward to take her arm in a firm grasp. "We have guests to whom we should be paying attention! I will tell you now, however, that I don't want to see you out for any more moonlight strolls with Matt Wentworth or anyone else, for that matter! If you had stayed indoors like a proper hostess, none of this would have occurred!''

"You mean it's better for you if I don't know what's going on behind my back?'' Phoebe turned a fulminating look up at him.

"I mean there's less likelihood of misinterpretation if you aren't out wandering around where you shouldn't be!'' he snapped.

"Oh! You're being horribly unfair, Harlan!''

"I am a little upset over having had a long-time friend of mine tossed into a fish pond! And about finding my future wife on a moonlight ramble with Matt Wentworth! If that constitutes being unfair, then, yes, I'm unfair! That doesn't change matters, however! You're going to learn to behave yourself, Phoebe, if it takes me the rest of my life to teach you!''

Before she could say another word in her own defense, they were crossing the terrace and Phoebe was being thrust back through the open doors into the living room. The sudden necessity of facing a great many smilingly curious guests forced her to exert her self-control, but she managed.

Phoebe wasn't at all certain how she got through the rest of the evening. It took every ounce of will power and stamina she possessed. She would never afterward be able to say exactly what she discussed that night, but no one seemed to have any inkling of what she was going through. She was accepted graciously into the Garand social world and Florence Garand beamed as if a great triumph had been accomplished.

"Phoebe, you were marvelous!" Flo enthused after everyone, including Steve, had left. "Mr. Cornwall and Hugh Ripley both made a point of telling me you have a real head on your shoulders! They said you were going to be a fine asset to the Garand family. And Bertha Hargate said she thought you were the most charming creature she's met in a long time. I'm telling you I received nothing but praise all evening long. So did Harlan! I kept hearing the men say how lucky he was!"

"Did anyone get Cynthia Prescott's opinion?" Phoebe asked sadly, watching Harlan come toward them from seeing off the final departure.

"That woman? I didn't even invite her!" Flo said in surprise.

"She was here. I threw her into the fish pond," Phoebe stated. Better get the whole truth out in the open.

Florence stared at her for a second and then burst out laughing. "I couldn't have greeted her better myself! The fish pond is exactly where she belonged!"

"Regardless of your opnions on the woman, I won't have Phoebe making a practice out of assaulting anyone she happens to take a dislike to!" Harlan announced determinedly.

"Don't worry, I won't bother any more of your old

friends!" Phoebe got out. "You can spend as much time disappearing into gardens with them as you want! Now, if you will both excuse me, I'm going to bed! Goodnight, Flo. Thank you for a very lovely party!" With a dignified flounce, Phoebe lifted her chin and moved toward the staircase.

"Phoebe, I'm not finished talking to you!" Harlan called warningly, but he was cut off by Flo's quiet comment which Phoebe couldn't hear.

Phoebe sailed up the staircase, down the hall, and into her room—only to collapse on the huge bed as soon as the door was safely shut behind her. Ferd chirped curiously from beneath his cage cover.

"Never mind, Ferd. It's a long story and I don't feel like going into it at the moment," she told him, depressed. What was she to do? Unseeingly, Phoebe stared down at the glowing emerald on her finger. She couldn't tolerate life with Harlan if he was going to humiliate her as he had this evening, Phoebe told herself resolutely. The way he had allowed that woman to . . . to curl herself over him! It was disgraceful! But, then, they were old friends, weren't they? How many other old friends did Harlan have hanging around? How many other women knew where he hid the key to his home? Face it, Phoebe girl, she lectured herself grimly. You've fallen in love with a man who's every woman's dream. And every woman was going to want him! How could she, Phoebe Hampton, hope to hold him in the face of serious competition?

Phoebe got slowly to her feet and began changing her clothes. She had her bag packed and Ferd ready to travel. She was waiting in the darkness of her room when Harlan's footsteps sounded outside her door. She held her breath, waiting to see if he would pause and knock or move on to his own room.

He hesitated. She could almost feel him lift a hand to knock and then he moved off determinedly down the hall. Phoebe sat waiting, rubbing the palms of her damp hands on the material of her jeans. She needed to get out of this house tonight. Needed to think. She would go back to her own apartment.

An hour passed and finally Phoebe decided it was safe to depart. Checking to make certain the note she had left for Flo was in place on the dresser, she opened the door carefully, having a little difficulty hanging onto Ferd's cage and the small suitcase at the same time. Soundlessly she moved out into the hall and began descending the stairs. A dark shape came forward to meet her as she stepped off the last stair tread.

"Quiet, Jinx! You'll wake everyone! That's a good dog. No, you can't say farewell to Ferd! Sit!" she hissed and was gratified as the well-trained animal obediently sat, ears cocked alertly as she hurried toward the front door. An instant later she was outside in the cool night air. It was going to be a nippy walk down the hill, Phoebe decided, thinking she would dig the sweater out of the suitcase as soon as she was out of sight of the house.

She started walking. At least it was downhill, she told herself with a small attempt at humor. She seemed to spend a lot of time hiking these days—surprising since she had never considered herself particularly athletic!

A car or two trundled by. Phoebe stepped into the bushes when they did so, not wanting to have to deal with offers of a ride from strangers. Several minutes passed and then another car's engine growled behind her. Clutching Ferd's cage carefully, she eyed the terrain at the side of the road, preparing to step behind a convenient tree or hedge. But this car was traveling awfully fast . . .

Before she could find suitable shelter the vehicle roared into sight around a curve in the road. Harlan's Jaguar! The brilliant headlights fell directly on her as she stood helplessly holding the cage and her bag. Then the car was brought to a screeching halt beside her, pebbles spitting evilly out from under the tires. Instantly the driver's door slammed and Harlan was out of the car and moving toward her. She had time only to grasp that he had dressed rather hurriedly in jeans and a familiar looking workshirt and then he was on her, all outraged male.

"Where the hell do you think you're going at this time of night?" he bit out furiously, grabbing the bag out of her unresisting hand and yanking Phoebe toward him. The commotion set Ferd to grumbling as he struggled to keep his perch inside the cage. Life had been difficult for him lately.

"I'm going home! I want to do some thinking, Harlan!"

"You're home when you're with me! Haven't you learned that yet? Get in the car! I'll take you *home*!" he snarled.

"I want to go back to my own apartment!" Phoebe protested, struggling uselessly against his painful grip. "Not to your aunt's place!"

"I told you I would take you home, Phoebe, not to Aunt Flo's. It's about time we celebrated our engagement properly! I've finally learned my lesson, woman! I should have known better than to let you talk me out of making love to you Saturday night. But to compound the error by letting you talk me into this ridiculous courtship was inexcusable! Tonight you won't begin to have enough words to talk yourself out of where you belong! In my bed!"

chapter nine

Harlan was right about one thing, Phoebe thought wryly as she sat huddled in the corner of the car with Ferd's cage on her lap. She definitely did not have enough words tonight! Her few pitiful efforts at reasoning with him failed utterly as they collided with the atmosphere of stony determination which permeated the vehicle.

"How . . . how did you know I had left?" she tried finally.

"Jinx came to my door whining. When I got up to see what was wrong I found you were gone," Harlan responded shortly.

"That wretched dog! He just wants Ferd back!" Phoebe bit her lip in frustrated anger.

"He had the sense to know I'd want you back, too!" Harlan informed her coolly.

"Where are we going?" Phoebe demanded suddenly, realizing they had turned off the main road.

"Home. I told you."

"But this is the road to your house!" Phoebe muttered nervously.

"That's what I said. Home."

"Harlan, I'm not going to your place! I refuse! I thought you were taking me back to my apartment . . ."

"Shut up, Phoebe."

"You can't kidnap me like this! I won't stand for it!" she blazed.

HERE TO END

"Calm down, honey. You're getting yourself all worked up . . ."

"You bet I am! I won't be taken to your home and *raped*!"

"You'd rather I raped you at your place?" He inquired laconically.

"No! I mean, I don't intend to let you . . ."

"You're not going to have anything to say in the matter except to tell me how much you love me!" he interrupted unfeelingly.

"Never!" she vowed between clenched teeth, wishing she dared throw open the car door and leap to freedom. But the Jag was moving too fast. She would only succeed in seriously hurting herself.

"Harlan, please! Can't we talk this over? This is a serious step and . . ."

"Talking with you has only made things more difficult," he told her as he swung the Jag into the drive and switched off the engine. "I'm going to try another technique tonight. Stop looking at me as if your world was coming to an end, for God's sake!" He opened his door with a violent movement and climbed out rapidly, coming around to her side of the car at once.

"Here, give me that bird." He reached into the car and plucked the cage off her lap. "Out you get, Phoebe."

Without a word, Phoebe stepped out of the car as if she were walking on eggs. Numbly she allowed herself to be led to the front door of Harlan's home and pushed gently inside.

"The bedroom is down that hall, Phoebe," he prodded as she came to a halt just over the threshold. Harlan set Ferd's cage down, ignoring the indignant chirp from within and turned to lock the door behind him.

"If you think I'm going to go meekly down that hall and wait for you in bed, you've got another thought coming!" Phoebe finally found the courage to snap, spinning to face him.

He secured the door and stepped toward her purposefully. Phoebe immediately moved backward in a futile gesture of self-defense. But he was much too swift and an instant later she was swung high into his arms.

"Put me down!" she stormed, scrambling helplessly with her hands, trying to dislodge his grip. But the blue eyes flamed down on her and she recognized the desire burning there. It made her weak and stirred her own blood.

"Harlan . . ."

Not bothering to reply to the poignant note in her voice, he strode down the hall as if she were weightless, kicked open the door to his bedroom with one booted foot and carried her inside. Setting her on her feet, he pulled her into his arms and covered her shocked mouth with his own. His arms closed around her like steel bands, holding her firmly in place for his kiss.

"Don't fight me, sweetheart!" he ground against her teeth. "I know you want me, too. It's going to be all right, I swear it!" His lips became gentle as she surrendered involuntarily to the power of his embrace. It wasn't fair, Phoebe thought wildly. She shouldn't allow him so much control, so much dominance over her emotions! She struggled for words, words which had kept him from making love to her fully on previous occasions, but even as she tried to think, Phoebe knew it would be hopeless. He was in a new and different mood this time. Unswervable, determined, driven by a thirst for her which she could feel in the pounding of his heart and the fierceness of his hold.

His very need of her was seductive. Phoebe felt a

totally feminine response that knew no logic, only a desire to satisfy his hunger for her. Dimly she felt her arms move up to encircle his neck and his strong hands instantly took advantage of her unprotected breasts, moving around to cup them, stroke them, claim them.

"My woman," Harlan breathed. "My Phoebe." His fingers went to work on the buttons of her shirt, halting now and then as they progressed downward to touch and smooth the skin of her upper breasts and then of her waist.

"Harlan!" she breathed, "Please be sure! Oh, please, please be sure! I couldn't stand it if you changed your mind in the morning!"

"Change my mind! When all I've been able to think about all week is how much I want you? I don't think I could ever get my fill of you! So soft and so womanly . . ." His words were lost as he buried his face in the thickness of her shining hair, found the tip of an ear, and then trailed down her throat in a slow, sensuous movement which made Phoebe shiver in expectation.

Phoebe felt herself lifted once more and settled gently in the middle of the bed. She watched him, sea eyes glowing with her love as he peeled off his shirt and stepped out of the jeans. Then the lean, hard body was beside her and he was reaching out to anchor her closely against the length of him.

Outside the massed windows and far down the hill the lights of Portland gleamed. In the moonlit room Phoebe looked up into Harlan's tense face and automatically lifted a hand to smooth the lines around his mouth.

"Phoebe?" he whispered, capturing her fingers in a tight hold and pressing them against his cheek. "You do love me, don't you? I want to hear you say it. I know it, but I want to hear it!"

169

"How do you know it, Harlan Garand?" She smiled gently. "What makes you so very sure?"

His grin flashed briefly in the dark and he hugged her closer. "Because you're so strong, honey. Much too strong to ever let yourself be bullied by a man if you didn't love him!"

"You admit it!" she groaned. "You admit you've been running me ragged? Ordering me about, telling me I'm going to marry you regardless of how I felt about it? Of all the nerve!"

"You deserved it. You turned my whole world upside down and now I'm going to do the same to yours!" He removed the tortoiseshell glasses, setting them on a stand beside the wide bed and then slowly and deliberately unfastened her bra, letting the fullness of her tumble into his hand.

Harlan lowered his mouth to the tips of her breasts, tugging gently at the nipples until they hardened in desire. His hand slid into the valley of her waist and up the curve of her hip. Then his fingers slid inside the waistband of her jeans and moved down to the clasp.

Phoebe moaned as he slipped off the remainder of her clothing, leaving her naked in his arms. Slowly, insistently, lingeringly his fingers stroked her smooth skin from her breasts to the dampening, secret place between her thighs until at last her legs parted for him.

"Tell me how you want me, Phoebe," he muttered huskily. "Tell me that you love me!"

"You said you knew," she protested in a small whimper, some small part of her mind unwilling to make the final surrender.

"Tell me!" he growled, his fingers tracing circles along the exquisitely sensitive skin of her inner thigh.

Phoebe gasped and buried her face in the hardness of his shoulder. She knew then that Harlan wouldn't take her unless she told him she wanted him. As aroused as he was tonight, there would be no rape. Just as she had known there was no brutality in him that first night. She could stop him now if she wished. All she had to say was no and mean it.

"I love you, Harlan. I want to belong to you completely!" The words were whispered into the sleek muscle of his shoulder and she felt it tense in response.

"You will, Phoebe," he swore. "You will!"

She felt him move, lifting himself, turning her so that she was beneath him, and then lowering the full weight of his body on her. The hard muscles of his thighs found a place between the satiny smoothness of her legs, making Phoebe feel deliciously defenseless. She wrapped eager arms around his chest, clasping him to her with an urgency that made him groan aloud his male need. Delighted with this response, she began to work her fingers down the length of his back. His breath came more quickly and she felt a tremor go through him.

"Come to me, Phoebe," he husked. "Give yourself to me, my darling."

"Yes, Harlan. I'm yours!" she responded in a tiny, quivering voice.

Suddenly his hardness was pressing fiercely between her legs, demanding admittance to the sweet, dark, hot place inside her and she could no more have denied him than she could have forbidden the earth to turn. She belonged to him and knew it completely, in every part of her, as he took her with the full force of his passion.

"I love you," she breathed as he forced her to move with him respond to him fully.

"Phoebe my darling, my own sweet darling!" His hands held her so tightly as if afraid even in that moment of total possession she would flee him.

Phoebe's desire flared to meet his and together they

ascended the heights, hovered in an enchanted realm, and then leaped into space, finding for an instant the white heat of a sun before tumbling slowly, slowly back to earth.

For a long time after their descent, Harlan remained where he was, covering her soft, rounded body with his. He held her tightly, his lips pressed against the hollow of her shoulder. Gradually he seemed to regain his breath and his heart slowed to its normal strong, steady beat.

"You must promise me that you'll never, ever run from me again, Phoebe," he ordered heavily.

Phoebe smiled, gazing up at the beamed ceiling and feeing incredibly lighthearted.

"Oh, I don't know if I want to promise anything so rash, Harlan. Look where running away got me this time!"

"Phoebe!" There was no humor in his voice and she realized hers had been misplaced. He was in no mood for jokes, it appeared. Instantly she sobered.

"Yes, Harlan," she murmured obediently. "I swear I won't ever run away again."

"My God, woman! Don't let me ever hear you joke about it! Do you know how I suffered tonight when I found that damn note on your dresser? I could cheerfully have throttled you!"

"Instead you made love to me! Much more pleasant!" she smiled dreamily up at him as he raised his head to meet her eyes.

"When I saw you standing beside the road, holding that bird cage in one hand and the suitcase in the other, and looking so forlorn, I didn't know whether to read you the riot act or hold you in my arms and let you cry."

"So you chose to yell at me!"

"I did not yell at you! I thought I was very restrained,

under the circumstances!''

"You call threatening to rape me being restrained?" she chuckled, kneading the column of his neck with the tips of her fingers.

His mouth softened and the corners lifted slightly. "I only knew I had to have you. After you pushed Cynthia into the fish pond and I realized for certain that you loved me, I could hardly wait for the party to be over. I fully intended to come to your room tonight and make you tell me what you felt for me."

"You were going to make love to me right there in your aunt's house?" Phoebe exclaimed, shocked.

"I know, I know, that's not the way things are done in Portland. But, yes, I intended to do exactly that! Then you took yourself so grandly up the staircase I decided to wait until you were in a better mood!"

"If you hadn't spent so much time bawling me out for pushing Cynthia in the pond I would never have gotten into a bad mood! What did you mean you realized for certain that I loved you after that . . . that incident?" Phoebe demanded.

"I know you too well, little one. You had to be in the grip of a raging jealousy to do something that outlandish!"

"I was not jealous!" Phoebe protested proudly. "It's just that she was altogether wrong for you and I didn't want her hanging around!"

"Wrong for me? And what's right for me, sweetheart?" he teased.

"You need someone who will be a good mother for your heirs, someone who has a head for business so you can discuss your work intelligently with her, someone who can cook . . ."

"And someone who fits me perfectly in bed? I agree. Couldn't have phrased it better myself!" Harlan slipped off her, nestling her against him and leaning over to drop a husbandly kiss on her forehead. "My wonderfully cuddly Phoebe! You're going to make nights up at the cabin much more enjoyable than they used to be!"

"Harlan," she began cautiously. "You don't think I'm, well, too *rounded*, do you? I mean, for you I would even diet!"

"Don't you dare," he chuckled. "I'll tell you if you start getting too plump! You're beautifully shaped, Phoebe, my dear. Nice, full curves a man can feel moving against him when you're caught up in passion! I always knew there was something missing with those skinny, scrawny blonds!"

Phoebe giggled sleepily.

"How about you, Phoebe?" Harlan went on thoughtfully. "Ready to abandon the tall, dark, and handsome types forever?"

"It's strange but I never realized how attractive redheaded, blue-eyed, masterful types were before! I'm a convert, believe me!"

"Good. Now go to sleep, Phoebe, my love. You can cook me breakfast in the morning," he told her with satisfaction.

"Wait a minute! What about your aunt! When she wakes up and finds us gone, she'll worry," Phoebe roused herself abruptly with thoughts of Aunt Flo searching madly through the house for them.

"No, she won't. I woke her up and told her I was off to find you," Harlan informed her, stifling a yawn. "I let her know we wouldn't be back tonight."

"Harlan! What will she think!"

"That we're celebrating our engagement. What else?"

The sound of rain woke Phoebe the next morning. She snuggled closer to Harlan's warmth and remembered the way he had awakened her again and again during the night as if his passion for her could only be temporarily satisfied. He had brought her to a wonderful new awareness of the power of her own body, she thought with pure, female delight. He seemed captivated by her, delighting in her response to him as if she made him experience his own maleness to the full. She loved him and he obviously wanted her. She would have his children, yell at him occasionally, cook for him, love him, and once in a great while condescend to clean his fish. Soon he would tell her how much he loved her!

"What are you thinking, honey, lying there like a tabby cat?" Harlan inquired lazily, coming awake to run his hand down her spine.

Phoebe stretched contentedly beneath the caress. "I was thinking how typical."

"What's typical?"

"It's raining, of course. Typical of Oregon."

"I've explained it's just a myth . . ."

"Take a look outside the window!" she mocked.

"Strange, I can't bring myself to look at anything except you!" Harlan laughed and hauled her close.

"I thought you wanted me to cook your breakfast!"

"When I'm hungry for food, I'll let you know. Right now I'm hungering for something else!"

Breakfast eventually got cooked. Phoebe, feeling great after a morning shower, found the kitchen a cook's dream.

"If I didn't know better, I'd say you had it built just for me," she told Harlan, setting a stack of feather hot cakes in front of him.

"Maybe I did," he smiled. "I built this place with the idea of making it a home, not a bachelor pad. That means that somewhere in the back of my mind was the idea of finding a wife, not a mistress. That reminds me," he added, setting down the morning paper to drop great chunks of butter on the hot cakes, "I'd better see about making arrangements for the wedding. I don't want you getting any ideas about enjoying the easy life of a kept woman!"

"Does that mean I get to go back to my own apartment for the remainder of my courtship?" Phoebe paused, "Which reminds me . . ."

"I know, I know. You didn't get your yellow roses this morning! I was wondering when you were going to remember."

"I knew once I let you have your way with me, my lovely courtship would come to an end!" Phoebe muttered, reaching into Ferd's cage to unclip his water dish.

"*I* knew that as soon as I had my wicked way with you, I could relax and start enjoying the good life of a pampered husband!" he grinned, watching as she filled the dish and replaced it in the cage. Ferd appeared to be content, for the moment. He mumbled occasionally to himself but other than that made no move to interfere in the conversation.

"About your apartment, Phoebe," he began in a more serious tone, munching thoughtfully on a bite of hot cake.

"Yes?" she asked idly, sitting down to eat her own breakfast.

"You'd better let Mrs. Morrison or whatever her name is know that you're moving out as of today."

"Today? But Harlan! We're not married yet and I have so much stuff to pack . . ."

"We'll be married as soon as I can get it arranged. In the meantime, I want you here with me."

"I don't know . . ." she temporized. "I'd be more

comfortable in my own place until we really are married and it's awkward being a full-time houseguest at your aunt's . . ."

"You'll move in with me as of tonight," he stated firmly.

"Harlan," she began, equally firmly, confronting him across the breakfast table. "I would prefer to stay in my own place!"

"You'll do as I say, Phoebe. That kidnapper is still at large and I'm not having you in that apartment alone. That's final."

He surged to his feet and stretched out a hand to yank her up beside him.

"But, Harlan!" Phoebe began in a broken protest that was cut off by his ruthless mouth.

"You taste of honey and butter," he told her. "I'm going to take you back to bed and taste every inch of your soft body. And you're going to tell me over and over again how much you love me. You won't be able to help yourself!" He scooped her into his arms and carried her down the hall to the bedroom.

chapter ten

Harlan at her side, Phoebe turned in her notice to Mrs. Morrison that afternoon.

"It will take me a few days to clear everything out," she explained quickly as her landlady eyed Harlan interestedly. Harlan returned the look with a wickedly bland one of his own.

"Moving in with him are you?" Mrs. Morrison demanded, waving a paint brush in Harlan's direction. "Don't blame you. Would have done the same thing myself!"

"We're going to be married, Mrs. Morrison," Phoebe said with great dignity, holding up her engagement ring. The emerald flashed in the sunlight. The morning rain had obligingly ceased around noon.

"I knew it all along. Knew it the day he brought you home," Mrs. Morrison nodded craftily, reminding Phoebe rather forcibly of Ferd in his more self-important moments. "Then when he up and took you off to stay with his aunt I realized it would only be a matter of time before he figured out a way to get you under his own roof!"

"You were so right, Mrs. Morrison," Harlan confirmed cheerfully. "Phoebe took a bit of coaxing, but she's finally realized what she wants!" He slanted a shark grin in Phoebe's direction, a grin which widened as the flush deepened in her face.

"You take good care of her, young man!" Mrs.

Morrison admonished firmly. "For all her airs of being a modern young businesswoman, she's still very much a woman!"

"I'm not likely to forget it," Harlan promised. "Or let her forget it!"

"Harlan, I have a great deal of packing to do!" Phoebe interrupted the embarrassing discussion desperately. "It's getting late and your aunt is expecting us for dinner. We're due to see my brother off in a couple of hours . . ."

"I'm coming, honey. Just wanted to reassure Mrs. Morrison here, you know . . ." With a deep chuckle he followed her firm little back toward the elevator.

Phoebe selected a car full of items that afternoon, sighing as she took a last look around the apartment.

"There's still so much stuff in here! We'll never be able to move it with just the Jag. What shall I do with all this furniture?"

"You could have a yard sale," Harlan suggested. "But save the fan chair. I've grown rather fond of it."

They carted boxes and clothes into Harlan's house until it was time to leave for Aunt Flo's. Harlan had obligingly and with a great show of enthusiasm emptied out several drawers, cleared a space in the closet, and given her a bath to herself.

"We'll shower together naturally, but you can keep the rest of your female things in here," he told her, throwing open a door to reveal a plushly carpeted and mirrored room. Phoebe ignored his comment on showering and glanced around with pleasure.

"You're quite sure you didn't build this place as a bachelor pad? You really intended all this for a mere wife?" she queried innocently.

"A properly gilded cage," Harlan smiled, but the look in his eyes was suddenly intense and Phoebe found

179

herself feeling flustered.

"I suppose we ought to get ready to go to your aunt's," she suggested quickly, turning to move back into the bedroom.

"I suppose so."

Flo greeted them at the door, Jinx at her heels, with a look of such pleasure that Phoebe, who had been somewhat nervous over the encounter, relaxed immediately. She had been rather relieved when her brother had announced that as long as he was in the vicinity, he was taking a flight up to Seattle to settle some business with an aerospace firm. He had left on the special hotel bus to the airport that afternoon, promising to be back for the wedding. Phoebe was saved the difficulty of explaining her move in with Harlan. True, it was a modern age but brothers still tended to behave like brothers!

"Something tells me this is going to be one of history's shorter engagements!" Flo laughed, bending forward to kiss Phoebe lightly on the cheek. "Have you set the date, Harlan?"

"I'll make a few calls tomorrow, but I think Wednesday will work out fine. Steve says he'll be back by then," he answered complacently.

"Wednesday!" Phoebe squeaked involuntarily.

"Any problems with Wednesday?" Harlan asked smoothly, flicking an amused glance over her.

"No. No, I guess not," she smiled tremulously.

"Enjoy the sensation of being rushed off your feet, Phoebe," Flo advised wisely. "I'm certainly getting a kick out of watching it happen! I consider it one of my greater accomplishments in life that Harlan turned out exactly like one of the heroes in a romantic novel!"

"Except for the red hair and blue eyes," Phoebe pointed out smugly.

"Which only makes the achievement all the greater!

Look at the handicap I was working with!" Flo laughed and led the way toward the living room. "Come along, Harlan, you can pour me a drink."

"Yes, ma'am," he agreed with mock obedience, leaving Phoebe to follow with Jinx.

"As for you, you idiot dog," she hissed, glaring down at the tail-wagging animal, "Don't try to kid me that what you did last night was for my own good! I know it's Ferd you're after!"

Jinx whined his innocence, dark eyes gazing up at her pleadingly. With a wry chuckle, Phoebe reached down and stroked his silky ears. "Why is it I don't seem to be able to hold my own around you and your master?" she groaned.

Harlan insisted on leaving relatively early, claiming he and Phoebe both had to get to work the next morning. Phoebe shook her head sadly at the door, turning to say goodnight to her hostess.

"You see how things have changed already, Flo? No more late nights dancing, no more yellow roses in the morning . . ."

"Nag, nag, nag," Harlan grumbled. "Come on, Phoebe. You, too, Jinx. It's time you went home. I'm sure Ferd missed your company." He bundled dog and woman into the Jag, leaning down to drop a quick kiss on Phoebe's nose before he shut the door. "Goodnight, Flo," he called. "I'll let you know the exact time of the wedding when I get everything settled tomorrow. Probably be around noon."

Jinx stood in the backseat of the Jaguar on the ride home, hanging his head over the front between Harlan and Phoebe.

"Are we going to take Jinx and Ferd with us on the honeymoon?" Phoebe asked laughingly as she scratched the dog's ears.

"That depends on where we go, I imagine. Can you leave the company early?"

"You mean, before Friday? I expect so. I've got everything in pretty good shape and it looks like the woman who has been my assistant will get my job so the daily routine should flow fairly smoothly," Phoebe said thoughtfully. "Yes, I could leave on Wednesday. Can you?"

"I told you, one of the advantages of owning your own firm is getting to do what you want!"

"I'm impressed! Maybe I should look into setting up my own business when we return from the honeymoon instead of simply looking for another job!" Phoebe smiled.

"You want to return to work?" Harlan asked a bit distantly.

'Oh, yes!"

"Well, we can talk about it on the honeymoon. Where would you like to go?" Harlan swung the car into the drive and shut off the engine with a swift, easy motion. Poebe climbed out, not waiting for him to open her door.

Jinx bounded over the seat and onto the gravel beside Phoebe.

"Anywhere I don't have to clean fish will be fine with me!" she told Harlan firmly.

"And here I was thinking I could work in another fishing trip this week!" he groaned, turning the key in the lock and opening the door to let Phoebe enter ahead of him.

Phoebe was on the verge of letting him know what she thought of the idea when the glint of moonlight on metal a few feet inside the darkened hall made her freeze. In the same instant Jinx growled a warning, sounding uncertain about dealing with a stranger who had already made himself at home in the house.

"Keep that damn dog under control or I'll kill him, I swear I'll kill him!" snarled a voice Phoebe recognized with a plunging sense of despair. The voice sounded vastly more dangerous than it had on Friday night because of the fear imbedded in it tonight. A scared man was an irrational man.

"Jinx! Down!" Harlan's voice was deadly quiet. The dog subsided alertly at his master's feet.

"The mysterious Max, I presume," Harlan continued calmly, moving unobtrusively to a point beside Phoebe and a fraction of an inch in front.

"Stand right where you are!" the slender, ugly man dressed in a black tee shirt and dark pants snapped, swinging the barrel of an equally ugly gun around wildly.

"We thought you'd be in another state by now," she whispered, sensing the tension in the man and dog beside her. Like a board meeting, she told herself crazily. Everyone so tense you could feel it! You had to get people talking. It was the only way to ease the atmosphere!

"I couldn't leave with you running around loose, now could I?" Max demanded in a high-pitched voice. "You had to be a fool and go to the cops! And we hadn't even done anything!"

"Not done anything!" Phoebe gasped in amazement.

"We just wanted to have a little fun," Max whined, sounding aggrieved. "But you spoiled everything! Threw that boiling water on Frank and then running away like that! I got to thinking about it later. I realized that with my brother in jail . . ."

"Your brother!" Phoebe interrupted again, surprised.

"Oh, yes, you bitch, I know you had him arrested!

183

He, poor fool, had to have his revenge and look what it got him! But I won't be so dumb!" Max announced proudly. "No, I'm going to get even with you for what you did to him and cover myself at the same time!"

"It was you who left Phoebe's window open Monday night?" Harlan asked almost gently. "You must have taken the truck and fled for a time before you decided to come back for Phoebe . . ."

"I finally found the bitch from the address in her purse," Max explained impatiently, sounding more nervous by the second. He'd probably never done anything quite this dramatic before and was trying to work himself up to it. "But she was gone when I went to get her that night. When I came back later she still wasn't there. I didn't find out until the two of you showed up this afternoon that she'd moved in with you! I was beginning to think I'd wasted my time keeping an eye on the apartment house!"

Max suddenly reached out and grabbed Phoebe against him, locking an arm around her throat and motioning Harlan back with the gun. "Come on, both of you. I want to get this over with . . ."

"What are you planning? A short drive up into the hills?" Harlan inquired coolly. "The police will find out, you know. They're tracing your brother's background now. Sooner or later they'll start wondering about you. You'd be better off taking your chances by leaving the country. Phoebe and I will give you twenty-four hours before going to the police. Time enough to catch a plane to South America . . ."

"Oh, no you don't! I wouldn't trust you for a second. You took Frank right to the cops, didn't you?" Max pointed out with totally valid logic. He began edging Phoebe toward the door.

Phoebe's whole focus of attention now was on

Harlan. Harlan who was as taut as a coiled spring. She knew he was and yet he looked as if being threatened with murder was an everday event! His eyes were on hers, she could feel him willing her to read his mind. Her feet dragged as Max pushed and prodded her in an arc around Harlan and Jinx toward the door.

In the dimly lit room Phoebe struggled desperately to understand the message from Harlan's brilliant eyes. He flicked a quick glance down to the gun in Max's hand and back and then she knew. She was going to have to do something, anything to throw her attacker off guard for a crucial second. She was the only one close enough to act! Deliberately she let her body go slightly limp. Not enough to make the man think she was actively resisting, only that she was terrified and finding it hard to move. Which wasn't far from the truth, Phoebe thought grimly.

"Here, you! Stop stalling! We've got a lot to do tonight!" Max's voice carried impatience. He was in the process of deciding how to angle both of them through the partially opened door and still keep an eye on Harlan. When he dragged her over the threshold she would have a small chance . . .

Max's body shifted a fraction. His arm at her throat didn't budge but he was having to move down a step with Phoebe held against him. It was now or never, she decided, and with every ounce of the muscled and non-muscled roundness she possessed she threw herself backward against him.

There was a shout as Max felt himself toppling backward with Phoebe on top. She felt a blazing pain at the side of her head as his gun swept against her temple. But it was an automatic effort to regain his balance that brought Max's arm with the gun in its fist toward her head. The weapon discharged near her ear, deafening

Phoebe but the bullet flashed away harmlessly, unaimed.

Phoebe was vaguely aware of Jinx's sleek black body hurtling past her, toward Max's throat as she rolled painfully to one side. A split second later, Harlan was joining the fray and in a matter of moments it was all over.

Dazedly, Phoebe struggled to a sitting position, one hand going to the side of her head instinctively to see if there was any blood. He must have caught her with the grip of the pistol, she decided blearily. Didn't that usually knock a person unconscious? Certainly it did in all the books she had read. Eyes burning she watched the world spin, saw Harlan climb to his feet beside the still body of Max, and realized he was speaking to her. Phoebe tried a small smile, thinking how tall he seemed in the moonlight, towering over her as she sat there on the ground. Would she throw up first from the nausea or faint from the pain? It was going to be close . . .

Phoebe fainted at Harlan's feet in the best romantic tradition.

When Phoebe awakened her first impression was that it had snowed. But it was almost summer! Rain at this time of the year in Portland, yes. Snow never! It took a few minutes before the unrelieved vista of white resolved into hangings, walls, cabinets, and bustling figures. Even they were dressed in white, Phoebe realized . . . a hospital emergency room.

"Harlan?' she whispered turning her head gingerly. But there was no blinding slash of pain at the movement. Only a dull ache.

"What the hell do you mean, she's all right! How can she be all right when she's unconscious?" Harlan's raging voice could be heard above the clatter and the sound of an incoming ambulance. "Why don't you do something!"

"Harlan?" Phoebe said in a more normal tone. "Stop yelling at the poor man, for heavens sake! I'm okay." She finally spotted him as he turned a startled face in her direction and then he was covering the space between them in long strides.

"Phoebe! Oh, my God! I've been so worried! I didn't know what had happened to you! All of a sudden you were just lying there so still and I felt so damn helpless! Don't ever, ever do that to me again! Do you understand? Promise me!"

"Yes, Harlan," Phoebe said demurely, trying hard not to laugh at the intensity of his orders. "Whatever you say."

"Oh, sweetheart," he reached down to place the rough palms of his hands on either side of her face, the harshness of his voice fading into a husky broken sound. "I love you so much. Please, tell me again that you're truly all right!"

"I'm fine, darling," Phoebe smiled up at him, catching hold of his wrist and tugging his hand toward her lips so that she could kiss it gently. "I'm just fine."

Wednesday afternoon, following a simple ceremony, Harlan stuffed Phoebe into the jeep alongside Jinx. He dragged Ferd's cage off the back, handed it to his aunt and the box of seed to Steve Hampton, and then loped around to climb into the driver's side of the vehicle.

"You two enjoy yourselves and don't worry about Ferd the Bird! He and I get along very well together! And I've got several days' worth of sightseeing lined up for Steve here, along with some charming young ladies I know!"

Harlan groaned beside Phoebe. "Poor man. Be very careful, pal, I've met some of those 'charming young ladies.' You'll find yourself in the same boat I'm in, if you're not cautious!"

"Sorry about the fix you've gotten yourself into?" Steve grinned.

"Nope. But I'm a firm believer in finding my own women. Don't let Flo coerce you!"

"Fee, fie, fo fum . . ." interrupted Ferd in a threatening tone, his beady eye on Jinx who stared back balefully from the rear of the jeep.

"It will be good for Jinx to get some rest from this creature," Flo remarked, chuckling down at the bird. "He's got that dog buffaloed!" Harlan twisted the key in the ignition and with a last wave at his aunt and Steve wheeled the jeep out of the drive and onto the main road.

"Jinx may need some rest," he informed Phoebe with a flashing grin, "but I hope you've already had all the relaxation you need! I'm intending to enjoy my first and only honeymoon to the fullest extent!"

Phoebe flushed and laughed happily. "Just because you haven't been able to lay a hand on me since Max clobbered my poor head . . ."

"That doctor and his instructions to let you rest!" Harlan grumbled good-humoredly. "Talk about trying a man's patience!"

"You made an excellent nurse," she assured him, reaching over to pat Jinx affectionately. "Right down to the chicken soup. Even if it was out of a can! When I think of how many times you climbed those stairs at your aunt's . . ."

"Believe me, I would much rather have been taking care of you in our own home but Flo made such a production out of having you stay with her where she could keep an eye on you and then there was your brother . . ."

"I didn't think Steve was going to be wholeheartedly

188

in favor of having me move in with you before the wedding!" Phoebe smiled.

"That wasn't the problem," Harlan told her.

"No?"

"No, I explained our relationship . . ."

"Good heavens! And Steve didn't belt you one?" Phoebe asked in disbelief.

"Of course not. He merely explained that if I didn't show up for the wedding on Wednesay, I might as well never show my face around Portland again!" Harlan explained with a ready grin. "As I was saying, Steve thought you'd be better off at Aunt Flo's too with a woman to keep tabs on you. As I was clearly outvoted I decided it was easier to climb stairs!" He laughed and then glanced across at her, the expression on his lean features sobering for a moment. "I love you so much, little Phoebe. Believe me?"

"Yes. I'm not sure it would matter anyway. I love you enough for both of us." Phoebe smiled at him.

"I could kick myself for not telling you how I really felt the night I made love to you. But I swore that when I found you that evening I'd make you realize that you were mine. I was selfish enough and . . ."

"Egotistical enough?" she suggested with a tiny grin.

"And egotistical enough to want to hear you tell me you loved me and that you were mine before I let you know how I felt about you. I guess it was because of something you said at the cabin that first time . . ."

"About wanting a man to be head over heels in love first?"

"Yes. I wanted you to want me with no reservations. Even without the assurance that I loved you!" Harlan gave a small exclamation of self-disgust. "Forgive me, sweetheart?"

"This is my wedding day. I'd forgive you just about

189

anything! And I do love you, dalring.'' Phoebe felt the happiness rise inside her. "I could almost bring myself to forgive those two creeps who picked me up on the road that Friday night!''

"Don't get carried away! Besides, even if you decided not to press charges, the police have enough on them to keep them out of our hair for quite a while. A real pair of bunglers and social misfits if ever there was one!''

"Harlan,'' Phoebe smiled softly, the teasing gone now from her voice. "I don't really want to manipulate and control you. Do you believe me? Do you trust me?''

"I love you, Phoebe. I'll love you and trust you for the rest of my life,'' he said, his tone becoming serious to match hers. "Whatever one of us does for the other will be from love, not as a result of manipulation. Agreed?''

"How about cleaning fish?'' Phoebe hedged, sea eyes sparkling.

"Well, of course, that's another matter entirely . . .''